Wild Order

SJ Clements

Amazon Publishing

Copyright © 2023 by SJ Clements

Cover design © by Get Covers

Internal Design by SJ Clements

Editing by Treehouse Editing

All rights reserved. No part of this book may be reproduced in any form or by any electronic or mechanical means including information storage and retrieval systems-except in the case of brief quotations embodied in critical articles or reviews- without permission in writing from author, SJ Clements

The characters and events portrayed in this book are fictitious or are used fictitiously. Any similarity to real persons, living or dead, is purely coincidental and not intended by the author.

Published by Amazon Publishing.

PLAYLIST

"Hold Me, Help Me" by Halocene

"Somewhere I Belong" by Halocene, David Michael Frank
and Lauren Babic

"Humans (Let Me Love You)" by Sick Individuals, April
Bender

"Honey- Medasin Remix" by KUCKA, Medasin

"Still With You" (BTS) Cello Version by Gabrielle Dela Cruz

"War With My Mind" by Crimson Apple

"0 (zero)" -English Version by LMYK

"gravity" by Maaya Sakamoto

"King of Misery" by Saul

"Lions, Tigers & Bears" by Jazmine Sullivan

"The meaning of love" by egoist

"Middle of the Night" by Elley Duhe

and more...

Find the full list on Spotify

Wild Order Playlist by SJ Clements

For my husband, my rock and stability in my life built around chaos. Thank you.

For those who feel alone in the world. I see you.

"It is during our darkest moments

that we must focus to see the light"

- Aristotle

AUTHOR'S NOTE

Wild Order has triggers for mental health survivors. These triggers either appear off scene or happen very briefly. As someone with mental health awareness, I take your well-being seriously and want you to know before diving in to make an informed decision. Fantasy of self-harm, a very brief allusion to rape, and torture.

Want to know a bit about the world... but don't want spoilers, check out the end of the book for The World of Wild Order for the general rules of the land and more.

TABLE OF CONTENTS

CHAPTER ONE — SCARS OF THE PAST

<u>MILANA</u>

My family had been destroyed. Not just dead but burned to ash before my eyes. Their blood spilled and soaked through the pressed earth. I ran as far as I could, promising to avenge them. Embers of rage take time to nurture into an inferno. One that threatens to boil my blood and burn my bones. Flames that will destroy the leader of the Desert Order.

Scorching sun, dehydration, and starvation nearly killed me when I ran from my oppressor, Desmond. The one who killed everyone I loved. My suffering furthered my bitterness until I could taste it. In the five years that have passed, I've learned that Desmond's hunters would do anything to find me. Spies lurked in every societal Order and even amongst the nomad Wild people. I traveled on my own and survived by never staying in one place too long. Every creak of a branch was my sign to move on and it *had* kept me relatively safe.

My luck caught up with me several days ago.

Imprisonment is more annoying than the thought of death, but neither will stop me from killing the man who took everything from me. Although Desmond is far away in the desert, his lackeys make him impossible to forget. Omar, in particular, earned my resentment. His right-hand man that hunted me relentlessly for years. While my hatred runs hot in my blood, the cool air around me in this dungeon keeps me sane.

Being detained wasn't what I would call 'fun', especially when I did nothing more than wander onto an Order's land. The stone walls and pressed dirt floor were dark, with water dripping in the distance and mice scurrying when I was left to the quiet. The cadence of drips and scurries kept me company. *Drip, scurry, drip drip scurry, squeak, drip...* For days that was all I heard. Catching up on sleep was an on and off experience, and as much as I hated to admit it, I did need the sleep. Being on the run for five years was exhausting.

Yearning for my freedom once more to roam the countryside, the plains and rolling hills. Climbing the treetops and sleeping among the stars, being a Wild, a nomad, was the most liberating experience. If not for the running for my life every few months when the Desert Hunters would finally catch up. Bothersome that was, but it was better than the alternative. Better to be running than Desmond's plaything. The thought made bile rise in my throat.

Years ago, when I was a small child, my *Gunna* once told me about the world before the Calamity.

"Sweet, Milana, it was a land full of steel and concrete. Cities of it with people everywhere. A steel jungle of everyone going everywhere and nowhere all at once. I was a young woman and had so many friends and yet none I would give my life for. The moon was only as big as the tip of my thumb."

"Truly!" I yelled in astonishment as I climbed onto her lap.

"Truly," she confirmed with a soft smile. "And it would come and go in phases. How to put this, sometimes we would see the moon and others we would not. The shadow of the earth would hide it for a night and then it would come out bit by bit until we could see the whole circle." My eyes were so wide with wonder, I couldn't even find words. "Now, we see the moon constantly, day and night. She is a sense of peace and warning.

"I wonder what other parts of the world were changed. Living in hiding until it was safe to come out, I had your mother in a steel fortress underground. I never left the desert, but I fear it is my time to go soon. The travelers of old told me that the mountains are larger, the animals more terrifying, and so much more. I long to see it, my sweet."

Footsteps invaded the hush of the dungeon and my fond memory, steps that were sure and steady. I remembered those steps, although it's been a few days. Lyron, the leader of the Eagle Point Order, approached while I sat on a cold, hard floor surrounded by darkness. But he was not the source of my rage. I had not heard of this Order before, and I've seen my share of them over the years. Most of the time, unless necessary, I avoided them.

Lyron's breath was steady as the silence stretched between us as I sat on the ground, leaning my back against the stone. There was no light, only the darkness and the sounds within. Smart, but harder for me to plan an escape when I had no idea what was to the left or right of me.

The first day I'd arrived, I remembered his stunning obsidian hair loosely braided down to his waist, a shade of the darkest blue, like a sapphire in the moonlight. Darkened tan skin made me wonder if he was from the Ocean Order, and amethyst eyes I'd never seen before stared at me in the candlelight in determination when he ordered his second in command to monitor me. Judging by the schedule they fed me, I knew I'd been here for a few days, at least. But then it was hard to know for sure since they only brought my food as I slept. Their servings were meager at best.

His voice was grave and calm, ominous and yet... comforting.

"You are a quiet one. Usually, prisoners beg for me to release them by now." His voice also had a sense of pretentiousness about it. Formal, intelligent. It gave the impression he was not to be underestimated.

"I enjoy foreplay. Nothing gets me going more than being starved and listening to your breathing in the dark," I soured my words, tapping the back of my head against the wall.

"Ah, there's the fighter I remember in the woods."

I wince. When he and a few of his men found me at the edge of their territory, the fight that followed had been quite the ordeal. Five against one was hardly fair, but I'd made it *very* difficult for them. Inwardly, I smiled.

"You nearly took out one of my men. Your will to fight is admirable."

Was that amusement in his voice?

"How's that one guy's head?" I asked, remembering hitting one of them with the hilt of my dagger.

"Still on bed rest. How's yours?"

I stifled a laugh as I pushed off the wall to stand up remembering when I hit the one with my dagger hilt, another grabbed me from behind and I swung my head back to connect with his nose.

"He should have ducked, but I'm good."

While not completely true, the dull ache in my head roared to life from time to time. He wouldn't get that from me, though. Feeling the wall until I found the iron bars, I leaned against them as I stretched my back. The pops and release felt like a cool drink of water after a sweltering summer day. *Bliss.*

"Thor tells me you're not an immediate threat. I have my doubts," he said, along with the sounds of clinking and creaking of the lock and key. "He said he would take responsibility for you."

My shoulders stiffened. The door swung open, and a light approached. Inching closer and closer with steady, quickened footsteps, I groan when his face came into view. Thor, the man who'd put me in a headlock and hit the pressure point on my neck days ago. A bitter bile rose in my throat.

My eyes narrowed as a corner of his mouth upturned into a smirk. *Cocky little brat.* When they first put me in the dark, damp dungeon, he asked me over and over what my motives were, where I was from, and why I was there. My response was the same. "I'm a Wild." His voice made my skin crawl by this point, his casual jovial tone insinuating he was anyone's friend. With all the Orders, it was hard to keep straight what land belonged to who these days.

"Our little Wild here is not a threat. She just doesn't like getting caught. Like giving a cat a bath. She's spunky but not dangerous," Thor said as I took a step toward him, ready to pounce to teach him a lesson.

"I'll show you a Wild," I hissed, pulling my fist back when Lyron grabbed my arm and held it behind me like a vice. *Damn, this guy is strong.*

"Don't make me throw you back in there," he said, his voice low. He sighed. "And you," he pointed to Thor. "Don't antagonize her more than necessary. You said you'd take responsibility for her." Letting go of my hand, he draped a piece of fabric over my shoulder. "Tie this so you can't see."

"You honestly think I will let this asshole have responsibility for me? You're as stupid as he is," I said as I grabbed the fabric roughly.

"The alternate plan is that you go back in here until you either die or go insane. Either way will not make me lose any sleep," Lyron whispered in my ear, low and foreboding.

Evaluating my decisions, I groaned in frustration as he moved his face away from mine. I complied and tried to find Lyron with my elbow to give a small strike, but he effortlessly dodged my pathetic effort.

I try to give myself a small space so I could at least look down. Unfortunately, the man is untrusting and pulled the fabric so that I couldn't have that luxury. *If he was going to tighten it, why did he have me do it in the first place?* He gripped my forearm to keep it at my side, and easily wrapped his callused hands around my arm. He avoids gripping me too tight, but the warning is there. *Don't run.*

"You're no fun," was all Thor said as he led the way down the series of halls. This place was a maze. I had no idea which way was which as they weaved me through the corridors. The day they captured me flashes in my mind.

I'd spent my entire life on the run. I knew how to evade. But that night had been so oddly peaceful, and I should have known it would all change.

*** ***Five days ago*** ***

"Milana."

Hearing my name somewhere in a memory, I opened my eyes to no one but nature surrounding me. Morning had come, and I continued to glance around as I stretched. A dream, but one that I did not remember, just a woman's voice. Calming, like a mother's would be. Maybe it was my mother's voice. I couldn't picture her anymore. Rage and the thought of revenge blurred my memories. I could worry about remembering my family after my deed was done. If there was any justice, I would be joining them in the hell saved for betrayal.

Remembering there was a stream nearby, I headed in that direction, knowing how badly I needed to wash my face. It would help snap me back into the present. The sun was cresting over the horizon, with stunning gold rays peeking through the wispy clouds. The short walk allowed me to stretch out my limbs for another day of traveling.

Reaching the stream, I could feel eyes on me. Kneeling, I cupped the water in my hands and splashed it over my forehead and cheeks. Droplets fell onto my loose, faded blue t-shirt and onto my torn jean shorts. My shoes had seen better days, but they were old hiking shoes that helped me tread the forest terrain. The refreshing hit of ice-cold water made me gasp, feigning to be none the wiser as I heard a slight brush against the foliage. Someone was trying to remain undetected, and they had the advantage of the thick cover of the woods. Standing up, I stretched, but I could feel them there. Turning quickly, they were right behind me.

A tall man was before me, with chestnut brown hair and crystal-clear blue eyes. His forearms were tanned and muscular, the veins bulging like cords beneath the skin, and he held a dagger to my throat. *Already not my day.*

"You're alone?" I asked, sick of being snuck up on. Obviously, I was losing my touch.

"You first," he demanded as he eyed me for weapons.

"I don't kiss and tell, sorry." Tilting my head to the side, I met his eyes, and they were narrowed. Despite his less than welcoming greeting, I didn't hate him.

"I heard there was a lone traveler around these parts. A few men back at the city had a few choice words to say about her. I would have to say, you don't disappoint," he said, not putting down his dagger, but smirking, as he tilted his head.

He liked games. *But so did I.*

"You know them? Your friends are rather rude," I stated.

"My *friends*," hissing out the word, "know to be more polite to a lady, and also that it's bad manners to steal from the Order. Seems they crossed the both of us." Narrowing his eyes, I saw that the thought of being associated with them made his skin crawl as he twisted his neck ever so slightly. *So, we did agree on something.*

"An Order boy? Not my type then, looks like you go on your way, and I'll gladly get away from any Order and those associated with them," I said, moving quickly as he kept his blade up and eyes on me.

"I'm not too keen on Wild ones myself, but you helped slow them down. For that, I'll call a truce if you'd like to keep your life." He was approaching me again, but this time lowering his weapon and stretching out his other hand as he sheathed it at his waist.

"I've had enough male attention to last me a lifetime in the last day. I will agree to get you out of my way."

This guy was too persistent to be noble, and it made me uncomfortable. What was so wrong with calling it a day and leaving me to my own devices? I didn't think there was an Order right here, but then my information was not exactly new.

"Considering you're on the border of the Eagle Point Order, I'd say that it's agreeable if you leave."

***

The conversation did not end that way once I jabbed my elbow into his ribs, just enough to put him off balance so he'd think twice about following me. Four men came out from the tree line, and I was detained for questioning. Turns out that was Thor I'd met, and he was all too willing to make me pay for his ribs. Lyron had given him the opening to knock me out by hitting the side of my neck and further evaluate my threat level once we came to where I was currently being held.

The cool air slowly warmed as we walked through the corridors. While I couldn't see, I tasted the fresh air as I took a deep breath. Musty and damp was not my style. If I could live my life in the open air of the wild lands ruled by no Order, I would do so gladly. Too bad that peace would never fully come until Desmond was killed.

Thoughts of him made my blood heat with anger. My heartbeat sped up as I tried to calm my mind. Lyron's grip on my arm tightened ever so slightly, as if sensing I was about to run. However, it kept my flame in check, something that surprised me. And I was not surprised much anymore.

Running would be a possibility, but I had no idea how far I had to go to the exit. Guards could be everywhere and nowhere. While I am impulsive, I also enjoy my body above ground instead of buried in it. These last several days solidified that desire. I would be willing to die once a burning inferno seized Desmond's last breath. Until then, I just had to wait until the right time.

Hushed whispers of curiosity buzzed through the crowd. My blind fold may dim my eyes' ability, but the hearing was as good as ever.

"Who's she?"

"Another Wild?"

"Is she from the desert?"

"Maybe she's another..."

Thor's commands boomed over the crowd so loud that I winced. "Come on, keep it moving."

The people departed out of our way from the quickened steps I heard, but they lingered nearby whispering their curiosities. The warmth of the sunlight left my skin as the air once again cooled. Despite my hesitation and digging my heels into the ground, Lyron pushed me forward. My head shook as my breathing quickened, shallow and erratic. My palms became clammy and cold.

Lyron slowed down and loosened his grip ever so slightly. My shoulders quivered as I took a deep breath. Not knowing where they were taking me was torture. If I lingered too long, Desmond's spies would find me. Just like these two had before being taken here.

"She's terrified," Thor whispered, sounding less than pleased with himself from what I could guess.

"We'll take her up," Lyron whispered back, his voice strained.

What would it matter if I was terrified? They had no business caring if they were less than reasonable when imprisoning me, they didn't have the right to feel guilty now. Too many men in this world had the complex that they were justified in whatever they did so long as it meant restoring the human population and protecting their Order. I only sought the right to protect myself with whatever means necessary. *The nerve.*

Stairs, so many stairs that spiraled up. A tower? I didn't remember seeing a tower in the distance, but then the dense forest would do well to conceal that. My journey to the Northern Order, a rumored Order ran by solely women, had been a failure, but all I had to do was escape from here like I did the multitude of other times I got into questionable situations. Every step made the idea less probable as I worked through every scenario. Until this cloth came off my eyes. I was blind to any telltale way to escape.

The sudden jolt of a dense wood door with hinges that ached to have some maintenance broke my thoughts. Shaking my head from the high-pitched noise, I was guided to take a sharp left. Lyron closed the door as he let me go. Whipping off the blindfold, I looked around the room.

A window was the only freedom I could see with two men currently blocking the door, but even then, the well-kept natural stone walls, floor and ceiling hardly made me feel comfortable. A slight earthy smell permeated the surrounding air, almost making me feel at home when I closed my eyes.

A modest bed made of hay lay atop a makeshift wooden frame. The small wooden table next to the bed was bare, and the wooden chair and round table next to the window had a thin layer of dust. In the middle of the table was a candle.

Walking to the window, the men gave me a moment to absorb the room. The sunlight was shimmering through the window frame. I glanced out at the life below me. Life was in every soul as children played in the market, with the adults laughing and trading freely. Wispy clouds blew by in the sky, the wind resilient with a broken moon hovering above. Endless hills of green and farmland spread out before me as field workers planted new crops. Every inch of rolling hills and forest beyond allowed me to lose myself in a moment of peace.

Lyron stepped toward me as I backed into the corner beside the window and the wall. He stops, keeping the space between us. His brows come together for a moment before he takes a deep breath. I looked to Thor as his hands ran through his air.

Lyron finally broke the silence, clearing his throat. "This is your room. We will have meals delivered to you until we consider it safe enough for you to come out." His words were gentler than before. As if speaking to a child. "Thor will show you around soon. Until then, just try to not cause too much trouble."

The corners of my mouth formed a bitter smile as I looked at Lyron. "One cell for another. At least this one has a view," I said as the men left the room. Hearing a lock click made me narrow my eyes. Of course, they wouldn't deny it. Nothing to do but wait. I sat at the table and glanced at the moon over the landscape through the window.

My grandmother would whisper stories of the moon before the Calamity before she passed away. There were phases of the waxing and waning moon, and it was as small as the tip of my thumb in the vast night sky. Understanding what she meant, as I had only ever known it in its current form, never really came, but the stories fascinated me.

The moon had a secret. Fifty years ago, war ravaged the planet and during that time, many thought that the gods were angry. A meteor came and crashed into the moon, breaking it apart and sending it so close to earth it covered most of the horizon. As it does today.

Communications dropped as things called 'satellites' descended from the sky and panic ensued. Nuclear warfare broke out soon after and it destroyed most of the human population, along with most of the animals. Only those in bunkers survived, and a few others.

The *lucky ones* were soon met with moving Earth plates and new geography, making survival even harder. What didn't die *changed*. Plants grew larger, and animals and humans mutated. Abilities and physical features slowly changed with every generation that survived.

For years, they said the moon was a terrible omen. Some now worship her, a goddess of the fallen for the Ocean and Oasis Order to the Southeast. The Snow Fall Order to the Northeast saw her as a guide to weary travelers. I saw the moon as proof that while one could be broken, they could still survive. She was a kindred spirit.

Standing up after some time, I poked my head out of the window and marveled at the sheer size of this place. I looked down below to the market, but the details were hard to see. I was up high enough to see the horizon above the tree line. This place is not a tower, but the highest point of a fortress built into a massive hill. From a corner of my memory, I had known a little about the Eagle Point Order before, only that it was heavily guarded and shrouded in mystery. Stumbling on their territory while heading North was only because I had no idea where their boundaries were. While the Orders didn't have a fence line exactly, signs marked the trees if a community was nearby. That way, travelers could make their own choice if they dared to press forward or turn away.

Bringing my head back inside, I flicked my wrist and fingers in the air to form a small flame. Rare for most men to have this ability, even rarer for a woman. Lighting the candle, I diminished the flame in my hand and the tiny flame danced with fragile pride. Hiding this ability helped me survive. After my parents were killed, fear paralyzed me as panic took over every time I felt my flames dance. Now, I drew from the flames strength to survive.

A timid knock sounded at the door. I pinched the flame on the wick until it wouldn't smoke. Heat and fire did not hurt me. Rubbing the soot onto my worse for wear cotton pants, I cleared my throat.

"Yes?" I asked.

"I have your food," a feminine voice called out.

She messed with the lock for a moment and cursed under her breath. I smirked as I waited. As part of me wanted to burst through the door, another knew it was too early and I knew too little to make this a clean getaway. No use in having two mad men chasing me or sending their lackeys. I only have enough patience to deal with one, and even that waned.

Patience was one skill that was not a strong suit of mine until it had to be. Trying to train on the run hardly allowed me to test my limits. I would not go back until I could defeat him. That trip across the desert would sap my strength. The journey was at least five days without a break, a week with some solid sleep. Part of me wanted to wait for him to give up and come here himself, but that was proving to be less and less likely as the years dragged on.

My thoughts stopped when a young woman, about my age, stepped over the threshold. The wooden tray she held had three covered clay bowls. Her hands were delicate and yet there were signs of callouses, much like mine. She was tall and wiry, her skin a coppery tint. Brown doe eyes looked me over. Long, sleek black hair braided to the side of her head fell over her shoulder. A smile formed across her face as she set the tray down on the table in front of me.

"Thor said you haven't eaten since yesterday, so I got ya some extra," she said, putting her hands on her hips and nodding in self-praise. "Sometimes they're paranoid with new people, but the way you laid out a couple of our men made them worse than normal."

I nodded, understanding the reason I was in this situation was my fight-or-flight response. I tended to fly too fast or fight too hard, nothing in between. The silence stretched as I opened the first bowl and noticed her fidgeting. Moving from leg to leg, looking around the room, looking at me, back to the room.

In the bowl was a soup filled with vegetables and a dark broth. The aroma made my mouth salivate. There was a sort of meat, scarce that, but still the delicacy of having a meal brought to me instead of hunting rabbits and birds was a blessing. Swallowing and clearing my throat, I hardly wanted to let my walls down and eat to my heart's content with a stranger in the room.

"You don't have to stay if you don't want to. Feel free to lock the door on the way out," I said with a long sigh. My forced smile to her widened eyes tried to ease the tone of annoyance in my voice. I was hardly used to company, let alone kept company.

"I want to stay. I just don't know what to talk about. If you don't want me to stay, I can go. But I gotta take the tray back anyway," she rambled. "There are Wilds who come and go, but I don't remember you. Sometimes Wilds trade with each other since we can't get around from territory to territory easier."

"I'm aware," I added dully. "I try to stay out of sight. Much good that's done me."

"Ah, I see."

The quiet stretched on as I gave into my stomach's begging. A small huff of air left my lungs, and I picked up the bowl and let the hot liquid and its contents seep into my mouth. The flavor was foreign to me, and I looked up to her, questioning.

The smile stretched across her face was not menacing, but calm and amused. "It's beef. We raise cattle for meat and dairy," she said with a small laugh. "Not many get to have beef outside of here. It's good, right?"

More than good. I didn't answer her, but the speed at which that soup left the bowl and cascaded into my stomach was answer enough. The meat that was there was shredded, so it didn't even require much chewing. The vegetables were also tender. I set the empty bowl down and wiped my mouth with the back of my hand before opening the next two bowls. One was a white liquid, the other filled with apricots and blueberries.

The woman answered my question with a smile, without me having to ask. "The white is milk from the cows. It's good."

Another new for me. I took a tentative sip and nodded my head in approval. Taking the smaller fruit, I slowly savored the blueberry. I put the bowl in front of me and slowly chewed a few more as I took a few more sips of the cool milk. I wondered if it was poisoned. I shouldn't let my guard down, but at this moment I didn't care. This was more food than my stomach could handle.

"Your name?" I asked.

The smile that appeared was bright and enthusiastic. Her body practically bounced with glee. Taking a deep breath, she collected herself. "Sorry. I'm Ivy. Thor told me that your name is Milana," she added, tilting her head.

"Yes. That's my name," I confirmed as she smiled.

"I can bring down what you're finished with. I can take the fruit bowl back later on. I know what it's like to go hungry and then suddenly a bunch of food shows up. Sometimes it takes the stomach a moment to adjust. Take your time."

"Thank you," I said. As she took the bowls and tray. I stood up and watched her. The top she wore was tied around her neck and around the midback, leaving her upper back exposed. It took me a moment to see an image that made my blood run cold.

When someone is a Firan, someone who can use fire, they have a signature of how their flames dance. Sometimes that flame is burned into their skin as a brand since other fire will not burn them. This was to show in the Desert Order they are of higher station when they are male warriors.

However, that practice soon turned into torture after Desmond took over. My mouth dropped as I witnessed that signature covering her shoulder blades and spine disappearing under her shirt. The swirl of melted flesh was a sight I wished upon no one. The act of it was excruciating. All that skin marred for life.

She missed the look on my face as she balanced the tray while opening the door, and it left me frozen by the table. My blood halted like ice in my veins. I ran for so long and for what, to have other people face what I feared. Suddenly, all that running made me ashamed.

"Get some rest. Hope you sleep well," she called out cheerily as the door shut with a thud, making that godforsaken noise.

Falling to my knees, I wrapped my arms around my chest as I rocked lightly. Neither sleep nor rest would find me. Hot tears flowed down my cheeks in agony as I slumped to my side, pulling my knees up to my chest. My hands covered my ears, trying to drown out every sense I could. Memories flooded back to me as I closed my eyes to see the torturing of friends and family I had witnessed all those years ago. The smell of burning flesh. The end of my innocent childhood.

CHAPTER TWO — SCATTERED HOPES

MILANA

Sleep eluded me for two days as I gazed at the omnipresent moon on the horizon and the sun danced around it from east to west from my small room. Ivy brought my meals, but my silence hardly made her stay for long. Looking at her brought it all back. The reason I ran and kept running.

Living with my own scars was one thing, but knowing I could have prevented hers is another. The cruelty of the Desert Order under Desmond's rule is ever present in my dreams. The same memory of my escape played over and over again the last two nights every time I closed my eyes. Even closing my eyes now, I saw it all so vividly. Five years ago felt like a lifetime. The night before I ran was the last time my parents and I talked before watching them die. Regrets would haunt me forever, starting from that point.

We lived together, ate together, and had no secrets. That peace shattered the moment I was considered of age to marry. What I didn't know at the time was the arrangement my father made was from desperation.

My mother was portioning up our wooden plates with a simple meal, a stew of desert rabbit and ground vegetables. Usually a favorite of mine. I eagerly reached out for my plate with a smile as we talked about our day. My father cleared his throat and said he had some news.

"Desmond has asked for your hand. I gave my blessing. You will go tomorrow morning," my father announced simply and proudly.

The shock jolted me as I dropped the wooden plate my mother had handed to me.

"She is so happy she dropped her plate. Wife, this is a moment to celebrate. Our daughter will make all our wishes come true. We will live like royalty," he said as my mother started another plate for me as my hands formed into fists on my lap.

My voice came in a hushed panic. "I do not wish to marry him."

"Daughter, are you well? I can hardly hear you." His voice was mocking as he laughed. The thought of being with Desmond made me ill as my stomach threw my bile to the floor. My body spasmed. I thought of the rumors of my friend, Desmond's latest wife, and how her body was found brutally beaten, and lifeless right after her wedding night.

"What have you done? Nerves? Clean it up," my father said, flicking his wrist dismissively.

"I will not marry Desmond." I was shaken but spoke clearly as I wiped my mouth with the back of my hand. I could not do what my parents demanded. For the first time, I would defy them.

"You will disgrace us. Do you know what will be done to our family?" His yelling deafened me, making me feel insignificant and small.

"He scares me! I don't want to be one of his many wives." A clash of plates hit the floor as my father lost his temper. Tears fell down my face.

"You have forsaken us, then? Do you know what he does with those who refuse him? Foolish, selfish daughter. You are no longer mine," he screamed. Desmond made us all afraid. Fear drove us to this point. I had to choose my freedom or my family.

I remembered how my mother begged me to reconsider. The soldiers came to our door demanding our answer. They had been waiting. They ripped her away from me and all I can remember are her tears. The soldier that held me down in my chair smiled wickedly. He was a man who enjoyed death, he was the one who would hunt me for years.

Desmond approached, his footsteps slow and menacing. Like a scorpion waiting to strike. His face was hard and angled, a scar against his cheek that had almost completely faded had been there since I met him two years prior. He'd killed our previous Leader. However, Desmond was not a Firan, but he had more than enough under him to make up for it.

"Little lady," he said, reaching out to touch my cheek. My breath became shallow as tears continued to flow. "I will not hurt you. Not yet. You have something I want."

He paused, as if waiting for an answer. I glanced at him, and his eyebrows rose as he waited. My body shook, and I tried to form an answer, but the voice that came out was hardly a whisper. "What do you want?"

"Your fire. As the only female Firan in this entire Order, I want you to serve me. To have you at my mercy. Your parents would be safe. Our children would be safe. No one would dare threaten this Order. I offer you everything you can dream of. If you don't accept this offer, there is nothing but death for you and your family," he said, cold and calm.

His fingers left my face and moved to the back of my head, pulling me forward. A whimper escaped as his breath mingled with mine, our foreheads touching. Tears streamed down my face and onto the floor. "I will ask you one more time tomorrow. Think about it tonight. I will have my guard outside. I wouldn't want you to think you don't have a choice."

That night, I planned my escape. My anger drove my actions in every way imaginable. Family was taken from me. The fear drove them to accept my fate as his wife, even if it meant my death. But living for my freedom would mean their death. My regrets would run legion, but I wasn't strong enough to defeat Desmond in a challenge for the new Leader. It was fight him or run until I could defeat him.

I chose freedom.

Executions happened regularly in the Desert Order. I remembered the hush over the crowd as Desmond laid out my parents' crimes against him and I was on my knees begging for him to stop, that I would be with him if it meant they could live. This was the day I learned to trust no man.

There was no mercy. Something in my mind snapped as I saw the blade run across their throats. My father's first and my mother's screams soon stopped as the same fate happened to her. Crimson blood flowed from slashed throats and soaked into the sand just below me just before the rush of an inferno incinerated their bodies. My eyes reached the bodies, unfeeling. Numb. Their faces I had known since birth. Even so, my parents tried to sell me to Desmond.

Someone pulled my head back by my hair, and I winced as the man who held my hair firmly brought his blade in front of me. Looking up, I saw Desmond. Twisted, arrogant, and an ego as large as the desert. My only fear was I'd never see his blood soak in the ground once I would have my revenge. What my father did was wrong, but what Desmond did was cruel.

"My dear Milana, did you change your mind? Your parents would give you to me for nothing more than promises. I took care of that shame for you. However, I have the shame of being refused by you if I let you live and you still refuse me. Quite a problem." He tapped the blade on my collarbone, inching the blade closer to my neck as the blood trickled down my body.

He loved to talk, but he had a weakness. An obsession with what he couldn't have. I smiled widely, like a lunatic. I used as much momentum as I could muster to swing my elbow into his knee. Knocking him off balance, I launched my head into his nose.

"I'd rather take my chances in the dessert," I spat, then ran full force into the crowd as they screamed. I heard a body fall behind me and panic ensued, no doubt from him throwing his blade in my direction.

My feet carried me through the compacted sand streets, the screaming and destruction rang out behind me. The betrayal and anger numbed my body and emotions. Escape was the only option as my feet carried me, ducking and weaving through the throng of people. A shoulder slammed into me, and I lost my breath, crumbling to the ground. Gasping for air, I struggled back to my knees.

As the air returned to my lungs, I felt my hand crunch as someone stomped on my left palm. Holding my hand to my chest, my feet remembered their mission. Hot tears swelled as the sand and dust swirled around me. I launched myself forward. One chance was all I had to leave this hell, to forget my parents and run for the rest of my life.

Down an alley, I hid from the crowd to look at my hand. Leaning my back against the stone, I winced, and I pushed gently with my good hand. Black and blue already and a bone not sitting right. Pushing myself from the stone wall, I carried on down the alleyway to the wall separating us from the open desert.

This Order—no Desmond—had destroyed everything I loved. Everyone I cared about. I had nothing here but torture and misery. The open desert would either carry me to the grasslands beyond or take my life. Either way, it meant freedom.

Breath became scarce as my breathing puttered. I slowly raised my hands to the stone wall that separated me from the desert. The smooth roundness of the stones made my hands slip. Their heat from the sun branding my hands as I ignored the pain from my broken hand. Fierce burns made the break more bearable. Looking around as I pulled myself over the top, I saw the openness of the desert.

Outsiders rarely came, and when they did, it was as if they would die without our help. The thought almost made me turn back, but death by the desert was far better than the death in store for me here. Swinging my legs over, I hastily clenched each stone of the wall until the granules of sand touched my sandaled feet.

I heard a yell from a guard at the gate as the deep sounds of drums echoed through the screams inside the walls. The gate was near enough to send my blood rushing back through my body, far enough away to where there was a chance of escape. They wouldn't follow me too far because the desert was a death sentence. Silently cursing and running as fast as I could through the loose sands as it gripped my feet, I glanced back. Two men were calling after me, taunting me.

"Crazy fool. The sandstorms are the least of your worries." He was running after me until he fell to his knees from the lack of stability in the sand.

"Let her die!" the second called out. "We will always hunt you!"

Yes. I'd rather die free than behind those walls! Sobs left my throat as I turned forward. I was never going back. I hadn't realized that freedom would come with many regrets. So much death.

Opening my eyes, I realized many things bothered me. Waking up in a cube bothered me. The wild world, open and free, was what I had known for the last five years. A window was my only freedom, but even then, the natural stone walls, floor and ceiling hardly made me feel comfortable. Even though to most this would be a castle, I felt trapped.

My ability to control fire bothered me. As a woman, the power of a Firan was never supposed to be mine. There had never been an instance recorded as far as we knew. Other elements depended on general regions mostly, at least from what little society knew so far.

People didn't fear them as much and found them to be useful. Terrans were the most common with the ground element. Men and women both could have the ability. Simply put, a person either had it at birth or in extreme cases a near death experience with tremendous stress, otherwise the ability remained out of one's grasp.

Aquan was mostly through the women of the Ocean and Oasis Orders along the Eastern Coast. The rarest was Airian. No region or gender affinity, but the ability to control air made most people afraid. Airians could strip away the air you breathed.

Firans were a mystery and the Desert Order kept to itself even in years past. To show my ability would put an arrow on my back, and I learned that early on after crossing that blasted desert.

My hair brushed my shoulders, and I finger brushed out the knots as best I could. My light skin showed the dirt of yesterday and the fighting that took place even after I washed by the stream. My golden-brown eyes watered as I yawned, stretching to wake up my sleep logged muscles. The memories of the Desert Order were bleak ones that I tried my hardest to forget. However, trying made the memories bubble up to the surface until they overflowed.

Shaking my head, I stared out of the window at the life below me. This Order was different. Eagle Point Order didn't run on fear and death, it seemed. Life was in every soul as children played in the market, with the adults laughing and trading freely. The many levels of this fortress were impressive on the outside looking in, but inside, looking out was just as magnificent. The clouds blew by in the sky with the resilience of the wind. Very few patches of sunlight came through and to only go away just as soon as they came. Endless hills of green and farmland were ahead of me where I met that massive creature that nearly scared me to death. Milking cows was a new experience, but I supposed there would be a few of those here.

I saw a figure below me, waving obnoxiously. Thor was waving his arm wildly until I lifted my hand in acknowledgement. His behavior confused me. Hardly acting like a second in command, he acted like an excited dog.

The loud creaking of the door behind me turned my attention away from the window. Ivy stepped in, holding a variety of colored fabrics. Setting them on the bed, she looked up at me. Her sheepish smile and jolted movements made my stomach sink. My mood had been less than ideal the last couple of days.

I sighed, running my hands through my hair and approached the fabrics. Her eyes dashed between me and the fabric as I lifted the top one, a dark blue with spots of yellow throughout. A separate piece fell to the floor, and I quickly picked it up. It's a yellow shirt that ties around my neck with spotted pants. The pants looked complicated as I glanced at Ivy's outfit. My eyes darted between her and the set of clothing.

"Thank you," I say, unsure of how to process. "They're beautiful, and they're all for me?"

"I can show you how the pants work. It's what many of us women wear. Easy to move in, but light enough to deal with the humidity of the summer coming up. I also brought a coverup for the morning since it tends to be cold yet. I wanted to make sure you were comfortable. Thor wants to show you around the Order," Ivy said as she stumbled through her words.

I smile as warmth spreads through my chest and to my cheeks. I nod as I listen to her instructions. I wrapped the fabric so it became a functional set of pants that could easily be adjusted for height and weight. She left the room for me to try, and while it took me a couple of times, the hem line fell to just above my ankles and felt dress like. I hadn't worn a dress since before Desmond's rule. The shirt tucked in at my waist and tied at my neck. I didn't feel exposed or over-dressed. Ivy entered to check on my progress one last time and she smiled her approval.

"You look so good," she exclaimed, lightly clapping her hands together. "I made them myself and I only eyed up the measurements. If you need more, just let me know."

I looked at her in bewilderment. *She made these for me?* I could understand her bringing them from someone else, but to make them? I felt overwhelmed.

"Thank you, truly. They're beautiful," I said as I played with one of the strings at my waist. "And I'm sorry. I haven't been very talkative the last couple of days..."

She throws her hands up to stop me and lets out a huff of air. "Honestly, I'd be worse if I were you. Who puts a lady on the top floor of a building with only a tiny window to see through? Barbarians, all of them." Her smile spread across her face as I laughed. "Thor feels bad, but Lyron is harder to read, but Thor is an open book. He wants to make it up to you. Doesn't mean you shouldn't give him a tough time because I have. Between bringing you meals, bashing in Thor's common sense, and making clothes, I've been terribly busy the last two days."

"Sounds like it," I agreed, letting out a small snicker.

Ivy approached me and touched my shoulder gently. "I like your laugh. When you're ready, come on out, and I'll lead you downstairs. No blindfold this time."

Letting go of my shoulder, she skipped to the door and closed it behind her, humming.

Part of me wondered if this was a trap by Thor and Lyron, but maybe just this once the world wasn't trying to hunt me down. Maybe just this once I could trust someone and let things play out without looking over my shoulder. To be as it was long before Desmond entered my life and ruined the idea of innocence. Deceit and death were two words that molded everything I knew for so long. I saw happiness around me, but never within me on my travels.

As I walked around the room, I felt the fabric swish on my legs. Memories of how I loved to dance come back. The Desert Order of my childhood was full of laughter and dancing. We were a communal people who loved freely and lived happily. Perhaps that made us weak, but we hardly ever saw the outside world except in trade twice a year. We made our life work for us, even if some days were harder than others.

We were once a passionate people who enjoyed life, but all of that changed when Desmond came. My father stopped smiling and my mother stopped her singing and dancing. My brother protected me as long as he could until one night he left and never came back. In an instant, Desmond took everything that mattered to us and everyone who fought back was killed. I was left to pick of the pieces of my life and store them in the deepest part of my soul.

Taking in a deep breath, I let it out slowly and raised my hands up to the ceiling before pressing my palms together and letting out my breath and lowered my hands to my chest. Doing this always calmed my nerves and grounded me before going into the unknown. This place was unknown, but I wanted to see it with open eyes. Letting my hands go, I looked around the room one last time before heading to the door.

"Guess it's time." Moving to the heavy wooden door with iron hinges, I gave a sigh before the loud creak resounded, announcing my presence in the hallway. Ivy was there with a smile as she nodded her head to the side, leading the way with a bounce in her step.

Closing the door as quietly as I could and failing miserably. There were torches lining the hall in an otherwise dark stone corridor. They were wide, able to fit three grown men, shoulder to shoulder. Not many people passed by me as we descended this fortress, but every one of them met my gaze for only a moment before looking away. It wasn't unpleasant, but more like a courtesy somehow. I supposed it was better than staring at me like an intruder.

The system of halls was simple enough, with stairs on the outside and halls of rooms where the stairs leveled off before descending again. Ivy leads me outside, following the slew of voices from the early risers. The sun was just above the horizon and the moon had a hazy blue tint. The quiet forests were more my home than this market of people.

Thor smiled brightly as he bounded up to us.

"I was hoping Ivy would get you here. Not too bad, wild girl." A small blush crossed his face when he said that, and I raised an eyebrow.

He was chipper early in the morning. His chestnut brown hair was wet and combed back loose to settle below his chin to his lower neck. Blue eyes danced between Ivy and me, as I took a moment to take in the outdoors. Finally, fresh air was all around me in the crisp morning.

"Navigating forests is harder than that, plus it's hard to ignore the noise." Tilting my chin to the group of people, before turning back to him.

"This noise is nothing. It's quiet now, just wait until midday. This place comes alive and there's noise everywhere. Right, Ivy?"

"For sure. I'll catch up later. Treat her well, you brute," she called out as she quickly bounded away. *Traitor.*

Concern grew in my eyes as I looked around him one more time. If this was quiet, then I would never get used to this. Children laughed as they chased each other around us, trying to sneak a glance at me.

The sneaking part was falling short. The glancing was a lot more like staring. He was no doubt entertained by my discomfort with that cocky smile I wish I could punch off his face. That would make a lasting impression.

"So, this is fun, but I'm already feeling tired," I said as my pulse pounded in my ears.

"Now, now, Milana. Just relax and enjoy yourself. I'll show you what you need to know for day to day living. Come on," Thor said, waving his hand for me to follow him.

Eyes were on me. Glancing around, I looked up to find a man on a large balcony and saw the raven colored hair of Lyron. His demeanor was different on the balcony. His long light hair braided back made him seem regal. I could remember the light amber in his eyes. The light color of his hair illuminated further his tan skin. The scar on his cheek was not visible from here, but I could only imagine the story behind it. Up on the balcony, he was a hawk, and I was just a mouse in a field.

Nodding his head at me, I nodded back before reverting my eyes back to Thor's explanation of the market area. Walkways were indicated with cobblestone, while many merchants lined the entrance's plaza with goods. Clothes, food, some jewelry, and small weapons.

Most were trades for other goods, but since I had nothing to trade with, Thor supplied me with basic items, holding them sheepishly as he continued his tour. However, the burning of eyes on me never left.

"What exactly will I trade with in the future? Makes little sense to rely on handouts." Frustrated with the idea of never being alone, let alone with a determined male.

His cheeks flushed as he cleared his throat and brought his voice down to almost a whisper. "Well, uh, that would be up to you, I suppose. The one thing we don't trade with is bodies. No slaves, no babies, no sexual encounters for items. Lyron has killed over this, so don't recommend mentioning it."

"Excuse me?" The harshness of my voice surprised me. "What in the hell made you think I was going to trade that?" My body was flushed with color. I could feel it in every pore of my being.

Amused, he stood straight and nodded before looking around. "That's what I wanted to hear, Wild girl."

"Why do you call me that? I get I live as a Wild, but I have a name. I've heard you use it once or twice. I enjoy being free. Is that so bad?" Throwing my hands up, I gestured around me. A few eyes lingered on us.

"The nickname suits you, and no. Most people can't have that much freedom without being driven insane," Thor said as he looked at me, his eyes suddenly serious.

I absorbed his words for a moment. Had freedom driven me insane, maybe? When trust didn't exist in a world built on survival, I relished being alone. Not that I always enjoyed my company. The memories were haunting and even I could admit my attitude was icier than most. That beat dealing with betrayals and death any day.

Ivy's back came into my mind. I knew that burn better than most. I watched similar torture happen in our Order's square more times than I could count. Desmond made us watch, to understand what was at stake if we betrayed him. Since he could not control fire, he made others do so. Those who had been warped by his sick obsession with power. Men who never would have done so before. Even now, I could remember fearing my own abilities. I suppressed them, fearing what Desmond would do if he ever knew. Someone had told him.

"Having freedom doesn't drive you insane, but the lack of company might. I have my demons. They haunt me, but they also keep me motivated," I said as I walked around Thor, ready to be done with this line of thought.

"You sound a lot like Lyron," he said with a chuckle.

I laugh in disbelief and turn back around. "How so?"

"People around here say, if you want a hero, talk to me," he said, pointing to his chest. "If you want someone who can make the hard choices, talk to Lyron," he said, wagging a finger at me. "But I'd be careful. Sometimes those hard choices haunt you. But I think you already know that much, Milana."

Looking back at the fortress, it looked so imposing. Stone embedded into a massive hill. There were no towers like I thought. They angled it with the curvature of the hill and flattened the top with guards stationed at intervals. I could only imagine their view since mine was similar in my room. They carved varying sizes of windows into the walls, and I knew the layout ran deep into the landscape from what I witnessed on the stairs.

Lyron was still on the balcony above the large archway. He was talking to another man and while I couldn't make out his expression or what he was saying, I could tell he was a very serious man. Our limited interactions also demonstrated as much. He took his job seriously, and I wondered what choices he had to make that would haunt him.

"So, that being said, if you ever feel you need to be saved, just ask your second in command," Thor said joyfully as he crossed his arms over his chest with a grin.

"Ah, you're that kind of guy. The one who thinks he's everyone's friend. I know your type all too well. Figured you must save everyone, right? When in reality, you save no one and everyone else is left to suffer because of your arrogance," I said with a bitter taste. My brother had been so much like Thor. So much desire to be everyone's hero before he disappeared, saving no one.

"Oof," Thor said, putting a hand over his heart in mock pain. "You know where to hit where it hurts. Are you sure you're not from that icy bunch of women up north at Snow Fall Order?"

"Can't say I've had the pleasure. I would have been on my way there if not for your meddling," I said, sighing, my anger slowly dissolving. "But wait, do they also call it the Northern Order?"

"Those bunch of brutes, nah," he said, waving his hand dismissively. "They'd eat you alive for breakfast and spit out your bones. Even we barely deal with them, and they like us. Snow Fall is a bunch of women in the Northeast. Northern Order is just a couple weeks' walk from here going Northwest."

Orders were weird like that, with so many alliances that change fluidly depending on who was leading them. Leaders shifted so quickly that it was a gamble from year to year if trades were kept the same. I hadn't realized Snow Fall and Northern were two separate Orders. Outcasts were used to describe them both. Perhaps it wasn't the worst thing to find myself here first, as much as I hated to admit.

"They keep Snow Fall Order hush-hush, so it's no wonder you didn't realize the difference. They mostly deal with the Ocean Order south of them, which is where I'm from. So where are you from?" he said, tilting his head ever so slightly to the side.

"Not here." I raised my eyebrows in silent warning.

"No fun. Alright, let's get you some breakfast. I'm starving," he said as he clasped his hands behind his head with his elbows in the air.

He greeted everyone he met. People nodded politely at me, and I nodded back, but everyone kept smiling. Were people that comfortable here?

Huts and stalls line the flattened dirt pathway that leads to the fortress entrance. Some stalls without a wooden roof have canvas lining the tops to shield from the sun. Everyone's smiles as they socialize while bartering seemed so genuine. I remember my brother when he took me through the marketplace when I was a child. The joy radiated from the people, and so did the laughter. Although Thor said this was not the busiest time, the people swarmed like bees to a hive. The sizzle of different foods radiated in the air with the intense aroma of herbs and spices. Metals clanking as a smith worked nearby, booming voices of bartering, and the lively bounce in people's steps makes me nervous.

Thor leads me to a stall where a man has his back to us. The food sizzles on a grate over glowing embers. Elevated on a waist high flat-topped stone, the iron base has an oval hole in the front to tend to the embers as needed. The man grumbles just loud enough for us to hear, but I can't make out what he is saying. Thor leans over the front of the stall with a beaming smile, showing his dimples as his eyes glimmered with mischief.

"Hey, old man Tucker, want to give this lovely lady some food?" Thor called out, making the man jump as he grumbled out some unflattering terms. The side of my mouth upturned in a smirk and Thor reveled in this man's fierce response.

"I aught to beat you senseless. My death will be your doing," he sternly warned Thor before looking at me, switching over to a smile. "Now that the ingrate is taken care of, you must be new around these parts. The name's Tucker. Before the Calamity I was a young boy and now I cook for these rascals. I got something good cooking up, so just hold on a minute. What's your name?"

He spun back around, with a little finesse, and he leaned in my direction ever so slightly. Most who were alive before the Calamity began are not as spirited, if they even made it this far in age. Fifty years was a long time. The radiation mutated much of our landscape, trees disfigured, most plants unsafe to eat for those who had not adjusted by now.

"Milana," I said, catching a lingering savory aroma coming from his cooking. The sharp sound of the sizzling intensified as he nodded a couple of times.

"Pretty name. Where did they get that one from?" he asked, glancing back.

My name was more eloquent than most. However, I couldn't find the courage to change it. Normally, I wouldn't say my name to strangers.

"It means favored. My grandmother chose it before she passed away," I said, not knowing why I felt like sharing that. I glanced at Thor, who raised his eyebrows and turned away for a moment while someone else greeted him.

"So, she lived through this hell long enough to meet you?" he asked with a look of sympathy as his eyes lowered to the ground. In that moment, I saw a thousand memories flicker through his thoughts. Many Calamity survivors did not make it long on the mutated world we live in. The younger they were, the better they adjusted.

"Yes, she told me a little about the time before," I responded, as my lips curved up into a hint of a smile.

"Well, if you have the time, I would love to compare notes. It'd be nice to reminisce if you're willing, young lady," he said as he scooped up what he made and set it on a small wooden plate. Taking a long wooden skewer, he stabbed the rounded pieces of what looked like bread and some thin slices of meat. Handing it to me, he smiled widely. "Let me know what you think."

"Thank you." Blowing on the layers of food, I took a timid bite. Savory and yet not overpowering, my mouth exploded in flavors. The hint of flavor from the tender meat made its way onto the bread and made me want to devour it whole. Herbs in the bread and the flavor of the meat wove together in harmony. Simple looking, but effective. "This is amazing. What is it?"

His chest puffed out slightly with pride as he came closer to me, so Thor couldn't listen. "It's my own concoction. I used to have this stuff called dango as a kid, but I did a little this and that, add some extra herbs in there and throw on some pork. Savory and filling, but easy to eat."

I smiled and nodded as Thor turned back around. "Where's mine, old man?"

"Ha, you had one earlier. I'm old, not senile," Tucker said as he ran his hands through his hair and went back to his makeshift grill.

A war of devouring and savoring raged on inside of me. To eat was to survive out there. Thor laughed at Tucker's response as he nodded to me. An ease washed over me as I smiled and covered my mouth as I stifled a laugh. This feels effortless, and yet guilt seeps into the cracks of the present.

"You did it again," Thor chastised, crossing his arms over his chest.

"Did what?"

"That thing where you act happy for a moment before looking all sorts of guilty. Like a dog that caught an animal but then gets yelled at or something," Thor said, shaking his head. "I'm not here to bite you. I just want to show you around. Loosen up a bit."

I take shallow breaths, trying not to kill this idiot. The side of my neck twitches as my blood pressure rises. I breathe a little deeper, walking away from him. I can hear Tucker insulting Thor as my steps hasten. Space, distance, freedom. If they don't come again soon, I will burn.

My body temperature continues to rise, well past what a normal human could tolerate. Thor's hand grips around my forearm as passerby's stare, hushed whispers dancing about the crowd. His eyes glance at me with concern as they meet with mine.

"You're burning up," he says, instantly releasing my arm.

"I'm fine," I say, continuing to concentrate on my breathing, on the canvas stretching across the top of stalls, on anything to ground me in this moment instead of burning every person alive.

"No, you're not. Come with me, let's get you someplace else without so many eyes," he says so calmly and quietly that I give in without fighting. I'm too tired to fight. Years of fighting, surviving, and death left me with a menacing distrust in every person I met. And yet I talked to Tucker so easily and I let Thor lead me back inside of the fortress. The thought of asking where I was going didn't even cross my mind. If he wanted to have me killed, he could have done that a thousand times by now.

Walking inside the fortress, the temperature instantly dropped. A cool rush sent release over my skin. Taking another deep breath, the flush that flooded my body dissipated inch by inch with every step I took.

Looking up, there were high arches that stretched into darkness. Faint torches lit the wide path under the arches, with enough space to allow hundreds of people through, and my eyes adjusted well to the faint light. A faint musky damp earth smell lingered, but it feels comforting, as if I were out in the woods once more. I miss sleeping under the stars. Between each arch was a path to a different section of the underground fortress, and I noticed the floor would ramp down then flatten. We go further down until Thor takes a left. Faint coughing echoed through a hall, not nearly as wide as the arched hall. The hall itself was an elongated arch that was wide enough for two people to pass and a small child in between. Coming to an open threshold, Thor extends his hand to have me go into the room.

There was a simple bed, side table, and seat next to the bed. Enough to look someone over, I suppose, for medical purposes. Not to house them indefinitely.

"What's this then?" I ask, narrowing my eyes.

"Privacy," he states as he goes inside first. I step in after him and he slides a door to shut the entrance. *Lovely... trapped once again.*

"Sorry, we aren't that friendly," I said, clenching my jaw, folding my arms over my chest and ready to charge into him if he had any less than savory ideas. If I learned anything in my life, it was never give a man the benefit of the doubt.

"Not... for that." His eyes glanced to anywhere but me, but he was frustrated at me for some reason. I wasn't the one who told us to run to a weird room in this maze of an Order.

"So, what then?" I yelled, not knowing what was going to happen. I needed him to do something. Scream, charge at me, tell me I'm out of this prison. Anything other than his prolonged silence.

He finally looked at me, his cheeks flushed, and his eyes glanced away again just as fast. "I want to help you, damn it. I want you to stay here so we can help protect you."

"I don't need protection," I said confidently. "You caught me on a bad day."

"That's not what this is about. Ever since you met Lyron and I you've been evading and attacking us, so we sent Ivy to help you adjust. We didn't intend to keep you in that room unless you wanted it. We just had to go through the motions of talking to the other guys you interacted with to make sure there'd be no hard feelings. We protect people here. The men we found chasing after you are not people that we want in our territory." His voice softened as he came a few steps closer, and I stepped back.

"The men after me?" I ask quietly, unable to fully believe it. "You captured them?"

"One of them—alive. We killed another, and two more ran off," Thor said, letting out a deep breath. A weight seemed to fall off his shoulders as he shook out his hands and a corner of his mouth upturned into a smirk.

"Then I can't stay. They will kill anyone to get to me," I said, feeling panicked, heading to the door as Thor grabbed my shoulder, holding me in place. "Let me go."

He did not. I tried to jerk my shoulder away and when that didn't work, my other hand holds onto his forearm. I repeat my order, only to have him ignore me. I dug my nails into his skin and as blood pebbles but he continued to hold my shoulder.

"You can go only when you don't run away in panic. I see it, the fear. If you go, I want you to go free of fear."

"I'm not scared for me, I'm scared for everyone else," I say as my stomach churns. *Liar.*

"Let us worry about our people. I see your fear. I see you. Desmond did something terrible to you, didn't he?" Thor said as he let me go and I release my hand from his bleeding arm.

"You know him?" My heart felt still as my body froze. Just hearing his name made me want to run. Although I told myself I wanted nothing more than revenge, I knew I was afraid.

"Stories of him, the people he hunted. Ivy, as I'm sure you noticed, had her own run in with one of the men who got away. I saved her from that bastard and I'm not afraid to keep you safe, either. Neither is Lyron or anyone else. Little did we know the target was you. I can't believe you're a Firan," Thor muttered, the last part so quiet I had to think for a moment if I heard him right.

"A Firan, there hasn't been a woman Firan ever in recorded history," I snip at him, trying to deny what he found out. *There's no way he could have known in one moment. What did I do to slip up?*

"I didn't just feel your temperature rise, it transferred to me, and your eyes turned from light brown to a flaming amber. I've fought enough Firans coming to do Desmond's dirty work that I know a Firan when I see one. Just didn't expect it from you," Thor said, pacing back and forth in front of the door now as drops of blood fell from his fingertips to the packed dirt floor. "But you don't seem like one of his lackies. You're running, you've been running. That's not someone I want to turn away."

My heartbeat quickens as I go through every situation of what this means. He could sell me out, he could tell someone in a drunken stupor one day and they could rat me out, or he could... protect me knowing what I am. But I was not a fair maiden to be protected.

"Now you leave me no choice but to either blindly trust you or kill you and run away," I said, squaring my shoulders up to him as he slowly turns and does the same.

"Ah, there she is. That feisty spirit. You may just survive yet," Thor said, appraising me as he puts a hand on the side of his neck. Looking at me, he smiles that blindingly bewitching smile. I wouldn't doubt if he had all the women fawning over him when they decided they were ready to be with a man. It was annoying how effortless his charisma was. "I promise not to tell your secrets so long as you stay. At least until you gather your bearings. If we prove to be less than beneficial to you, then you are free to leave. Just don't go in panic. I've seen so many die that way, thinking we can't protect them. We have protected any who need protection, and we will continue to do so. Even if you can survive out there, take this as an opportunity to rest. Rest and gather your strength for the next journey. If you stay, I will also give you the directions and who to talk to for Snow Fall Order if you still wish to go there. The best time to go would be in a couple of months. The weather is less severe there, anyway."

I was speechless. Opening my mouth to say something, then closing it again, not finding the right words. The deal he offers feels sincere. There are no feelings of deceit or trickery. To trust another person would require me to let him honor his word when I knew the world of men to be less than honorable. From my father who abandoned me to Desmond, who would rather see me dead than anyone else's, the men in my life who were supposed to protect me never did. Would Thor and Lyron do the same? No, I wanted to be free of feeling obligated to have men protect me. I needed to become stronger.

"I will stay simply to rest. Five years on the run will do that to a person," I finally concede as my shoulders finally slump to relax. His do the same. "But I will not be some timid woman that will swoon under your heroism."

"I would expect nothing less, wild girl," Thor says as he extends his hand.

I raise an eyebrow as I look from his eyes to his hand and back again.

"To make the deal final. I'll talk to Lyron and make sure we are on the same page. He said he will honor any choice you make." Honor surrounds him, as if he breathes that instead of air like the rest of us. I used to know men like him, like my brother, and yet it saddens me when I think about how every one of them is dead now.

"I'll hold you both to that then," I finally say as I put my hand in his and squeeze, equaling his for grip strength.

He nods with a smile as he goes to slide the door open again. "Welcome to Eagle Point Order, Milana. Please enjoy your stay."

"Yeah, yeah, but let's get you patched up first. They're going to think I enjoy making you bleed or just like hurting you," I say, pointing to his face and then his arm, remembering when I first met him in the forest.

"Wouldn't be the weirdest thing."

"That's gross..."

We continue like that down the hall after we patch up his small wounds. Bantering as if we had been friends for years. Those in the hall smile at us and let us continue our conversation. For just one moment, I can let myself be free of guilt.

CHAPTER THREE – ENSLAVED TO GUILT

MILANA

The next morning, I awoke in my bed feeling uneasy. Thor said I could wander where I like, but I just wanted fresh air. Moving to the outskirts of the busy market, I continued walking until I stood upon a small hill. I looked over the massive stone fortress of Eagle Point Order imbedded in the hill.

Dark, weathered stone discolored from the brutal forces of nature that pelted the region. Snow, tornadoes, and rain showed their scars within the stone. Countless windows carved from the stone and nearly all of them were full. Near the entrance, the market was lively as ever. Musicians drumming and singing as others shopped for herbs, fresh-caught fish, and many other trinkets. Many of the people here thought of this place as a sanctuary, standing the test of time no matter what was thrown at it. To me, it still felt like a prison, even if I hated it a little less after talking to Thor yesterday.

I heard footsteps behind me, calm and present. I glance back and see Thor before turning to look at the scenery once more.

The overwhelming structure in front of me feels out of place with the rolling hills, peaceful lake, and wandering farm animals. The laughter reaches my ears, and I close my eyes. It had been so long since I heard laughter from an Order. The communities were usually built on lies and fear. Obedience is the only loyalty needed with a Leader. Lyron respected freedom, but true loyalty was his goal.

"It takes a while to get used to all of this," he said, waving his hand in front of us as I open my eyes. "I hope you like it here, at least enough to stay a little while. Wilds are always welcome here, but it comes at a risk. Some of you mean well enough, but others haven't."

I couldn't stop the puff of air that escaped my lungs with an exasperated laugh. "I got that loud and clear from the conversation yesterday. Don't worry, I won't ruin your perfect little Order. I plan to leave after I rest."

The clouds overhead moved across the sky as rain was approaching from the change in the air. The gust of wind pushing me forward gently towards the towering stone building. Ahead of me, I saw Ivy waving at us at the base of the hill. Even as I wanted to believe this was not where I was meant to be, I couldn't help but wave back with a sad smile. *Why did the thought of leaving send a pang of guilt to my heart?*

Thor lifted his head and sniffed the air. Narrowing his eyes behind us, he put a hand on the small of my back. "We should go," Thor said gently.

I jerked away from his touch and pressed forward. Silence fell between us as I kept my eyes on the ground, taking in the green grass that swayed in the wind. He didn't walk ahead of me, only stayed close. Watching me was probably one of his duties from Lyron.

Ivy waved for us to hurry. "Hey, you two. Lyron is having us pack it in. Looks like the clouds mean business." Nodding her head to the sky, I didn't have to look to know it must have been dark and ominous. Even the clouded sunlight was fading away, although it was hardly mid-morning. "I just hope there's no tornadoes. Doesn't look green, so that should be a good sign, but spring is unpredictable. Sometimes I miss the southern regions. Much less drama for temperature swings, but hurricanes weren't exactly fun either."

"I have never experienced one," I said as she loops an arm through mine. There is no objection on my part as she ranted on how the wind, rain, and waves paved destruction. The ocean was always somewhere I wanted to see. The desert was an ocean of oppressive sand. The waters that I'd seen for rivers and lakes always make me feel at ease. I want to see the vast openness and not worry about my life as I remember the desert almost killing me all those years ago. To be hunted and reminded that the longer I stayed here, the more of a threat I became.

Closing my eyes, I felt the heat of the desert flood my memories. The agonizing beating of the sun as my body starved and dehydrated. No food or water as I ran to escape Desmond. Visions of my brother, Cyrus, came before me, mocking me.

"Lie to yourself all you want. You were always good at lying."

I could hear his voice echo in my mind. He was dead. The only respectable man I grew up with had been turned to the desert for going against Desmond. Those were the options: to die in the desert, die by his hand or his Firan soldiers. Just depended on his mood. That day, he felt *merciful.* Maybe that was what he felt he was being towards me when his soldiers did not follow me right away. Maybe not finding my body prompted him to hunt me all these years. Sadistic bastard never did like to be told no.

My brother was a proud young man, seven years older, and a natural born leader. Full of charisma and a smile that most girls told me they found attractive. His mahogany brown hair was often covered in dirt from training as a guard to our previous leader. Gleams of joy would shine from his dark eyes when he would tell me about his day. I missed that smile. He always knew when I was lying to appease father.

"I should take you to see the world. You'd love it. There's so much more to life, Mili." He would talk to me for hours about his time spent at the Ocean Order. Gone for months. I cried when he returned. I loved my brother, but even he couldn't save me from Desmond, so I wondered how Lyron and Thor thought they were better.

Looking up at the arch entry way, I couldn't help but lose my thoughts as I crossed into the threshold. The winds were blocked by the stones as we continued forward. "You should keep me company. I have a few clothing projects in my room that could use your steady hand and this oaf is boring once you get to know him," Ivy chided as she smiled.

Poking Thor in the gut with her free elbow, he swatted her away and rolled his eyes. Looking between them, I wondered just how they got to be so comfortable with each other. Yet there was tension as he cleared his throat.

"I'm not boring, I'm just busy. You don't know how it is to serve Lyron directly. Seriously, I think the guy messes with me to experiment on my mental state. Drives me nuts," Thor said, turning his chin up a bit in defiance.

"Yes, yes, so sad," Ivy said as she turned her attention to me. "Now, what do you say? Girls hang out kind of stormy day?"

How could I refuse? I nodded, and she escorted me down one of the many mazes of corridors.

Ivy led me down the maze of extensive stone hallways. How Lyron kept an eye over every person in this Order amazed me. However, usually an Order would have a leader, a second for scouting and safety and a third in command for overseeing the community. Lyron had made himself scarce from what I could tell, as he had not bothered to see me, not that I expected him to.

Thor was always around. Ivy was, as much as I hated to admit it, Thor's eyes were on me when he couldn't be there. The third in command remained a mystery to me.

The hallways bustled with joyful laughter as children played with each other. Mothers gossiped with a passing scolding to their children, without a care in the world. Some women stopped to glance at me before turning back to their conversations, but they didn't seem bothered by my presence.

Children danced around us and eagerly waved. I gave a small wave with just my fingers, and they giggled in response. The doorways for each room were spaced to give the impression that there was a lot of room, different from my smaller room higher up the compound. Some were a wooden door, and some were cloth draped to give privacy. The hallways were lit by torches between each door, alternating between the left and right sides. I could imagine changing the hundreds of these torches was less than ideal for some. The sounds of children's laughter reminded me of my old home.

How I remembered the Desert Order before Desmond was full of joy and laughter. Playing in the streets until nightfall and our parents called for us. We had communal living; everyone's house was our house too. A meal was shared with neighbors and clothes were exchanged freely as children grew up. Payment was unnecessary as everyone looked out for each other. Happiness that led to weakness. Weakness that led us to be taken over so easily.

Even with the Firans, the men used their abilities for festivals, and most were the cooks or blacksmiths of the Order. Firans were not built for battle then, as no one would cross a desert to bother us. Or so we thought.

"Milana," Ivy called out to me. "Here we are."

Snapped out of my thoughts, I smiled as best I could. Memories were harder to deal with when they were bittersweet. The door she led me to was covered by cloth with frayed edges. Pulling it aside, she let me step through to a room remarkably like mine. A square room with a bed and chair with a long table, cloth draped on every surface in a myriad of colors and patterns. There were candles beside the bed and the table that she quickly lit before opening her arms, gesturing to the room.

"Home sweet home," she said with a smile. "It's not much, but I'm usually only in here to sleep and make clothes. With the weather turning bad, I thought this would be a fun thing to do instead of you just sitting in your room. If you want, you can always come down to help me. Everyone wants new clothes, so I have plenty for you to do."

I looked around the small room and nodded. Briefly touching a vibrant green fabric, I smiled as I dropped my hand back to my side.

"Thank you. I may have to take you up on that. Sitting doing nothing is not a strong trait of mine." Muttering the last part, Ivy giggled as she took the green fabric I touched and held it up to me and smiled.

"I can tell. You're very, how you say, a woman of action. I heard you knocked out one of Thor's guys. Impressive. He's not really mad any more, just impressed. His wife laughed when he came home and one of the others told her a woman did that. She might stop by to see what your secret is. Her name is Sunny. The guy's name is Oak," Ivy said, bouncing with energy as she moved fabric from the table to the bed.

I shook my head, sighing as I remembered my skull colliding with his. The icy walls in the dungeon were great to help with the swelling after that confrontation.

"I'm a Wild, through and through, Ivy. That hasn't changed," I said. There was an odd emotion attached to it, a pull at my heart. I missed running free in the forests to hunt and provide for myself and the silence of nature.

However, the peace was always short-lived before I was found again. Desmond's hunters were trackers from the Earth Order south of here. They had come with Desmond seven years ago.

Kindness from men was a lure into a future betrayal. Thor's kindness was too much for me, but at the same time, it was contagious. I wanted to trust him, but many other pieces of me feared this Order, that man, and their leader. They reminded me of the home I missed. The home I wanted back so desperately.

"Wilds come here all the time. Some come here seasonally so long as Lyron approves. You could be like that if living here full time is too much. Have you even seen Lyron since they escorted you up to that room?" Ivy asked, and I shook my head. "Weird, but I know he's usually busy and tends to leave for periods at a time. Mostly if that happens, Thor is in a bad mood. Somehow, they run this community, yet they are usually arguing over the stupidest things. Kira, on the other hand, must keep this place held together. She's the third in command."

Ah, there it was. However, usually the thirds would run into newcomers. Then again, I wasn't exactly a willing newcomer. That position left the Desert Order as soon as Desmond arrived. He murdered the woman in cold blood, leaving her body in the streets as a message. Killed anyone who tried to move her and left their bodies there, too. The hot sun making them rot, the wretched smell permeating everything we ate and drank. Any activity we did was saturated in rotting flesh. Never had I wanted to cut off my nose so incessantly until that day.

"I hadn't met her yet," I said, trying to mask my thoughts.

"Yeah, she's busy with the festival coming up. The new moon is coming and we have a festival of all the eligible women who are looking for someone to join with. Children are sacred, but we don't force women to have children if they do not wish. Women who are ready to join with a man wear red, women who wish to marry wear blue, and all others wear whatever other color they wish. It just makes it easier since there are many women who live here. There's a huge fire in the square, there's music and dancing, food, and the children all stay indoors with the women and men who don't want to participate," Ivy said with a shrug.

I raise an eyebrow, curious. "Are you participating?" I ask, I hadn't heard of such a thing on that scale before.

"I'll attend, but just because it is fun. Not to join with a man. I think I'll make a yellow dress this year. I want it to be flowing and graceful. Maybe before winter I'll change my mind and wear red. You should go if you'd like. At least to keep me company," Ivy pleaded as her eyes widened, and she put on a pout.

"I'll think about it," I said, shaking my head at her childish ploy.

"Well, I'm making a dress for you regardless from this green material. I think you'll look lovely. I'll make it adjustable with a tie at the neck and mid back," she said, running her hands over the fabric as she beamed ear to ear.

"Do what you'd like," I said with a sigh. Taking that as permission, she goes between me and the fabric. As much as she said that I would help her, I wasn't doing much but keeping her company as her fingers skillfully worked with the fabric. What she could do was magic. My skills of a traditional woman were not particularly grand by any means. I could sew up a wound, not clothing. I could make a bow out of wood, not a toy for a child. The art of silence and staying alive was what I could do. My envy as I watched her grew so much that I ended up looking away and listening to the sounds of laughing children. How I missed that sound from home... or rather my former home.

Never truly missing something because there was no time to felt like a void formed in my heart. A subtle pain crept through my chest and threatened to bleed from my heart and soul. My hand came up to my chest and twisted at the fabric above my heart. Not enough to wrinkle it, but to keep my mind from spiraling.

"Everything okay?" Ivy asked as she glanced at me briefly.

Lying, I nodded with a weak attempt at a smile.

"Can you thread these beads for me? Whatever colors work, the more the better," she said cheerfully handing me a clay container full of tiny glass beads, countless feet of string and a fine needle. Well, this would be one way for me to keep busy.

Perhaps she saw right through me? And while a part of me was grateful the other felt uneasy.

I nodded again as I found a rhythm in it all as the pain subsided but never fully disappeared. Perhaps it never would. Guilt rolled into me in waves of differing strength. My running caused pain, but without running I would have lived a vastly different life. Perhaps one where I was broken, burning the world down for Desmond's power hunt. Perhaps one where I was too much bother for what I was worth, and killed for it despite my abilities. Desmond was always terrible at showing patience.

The low growl of my stomach as hours flew by gradually grew so loud, my face flushed a bright red. Ivy looked up and giggled as she set her latest project down.

"Dinner is probably ready if you'd like to join. We eat as a community here. I usually help cook food a couple of days a week. I'll show you down," she said, sliding her chair in as she stood up.

CHAPTER FOUR — TRUTH OF THE FIGHT

MILANA

Leading me to the halls again, we headed towards the way we came in earlier, but turning down a wide hall, much like the one that Thor took me down, with large arches and extra wide walking space. The noise gradually increased as children ran by, and adults herded the children through. Other adults lined the halls as Ivy settled us at the end of a line.

"Children eat first, then the rest of us," she quickly explained as someone caught her attention behind her.

I turned my attention to the details of the fortress. This structure was built to last, not elegant exactly, but it didn't need to be. The only elegance would have to be the arches. However, it was remarkable how the air quality remained good despite being underground and lacking an obvious ventilation system.

"Admiring the structure?" I heard a man's voice above me.

Looking up, I noticed the blackest hair I had ever witnessed. Lyron. He tilted his head as he looked above and nodded, as if admiring the structure for himself.

"It is unique. Especially for being underground," I answered, finally seeing him without being held in a dungeon or annoyed by his presence. "Many would find the structure misleading if they were to plan an attack."

Glancing down at me and raising an eyebrow, he nodded again. Some people took interest and sheepishly observed. "Interesting take. Do you think people would be motivated to attack or shy away?" Lyron asked.

"Hard to say. Some might be too confident but then easily overwhelmed if your fighting force is anything to be reckoned with. Or they would see the outside and shy away, depending on their strategy and their own methods of fighting. Also, it's hard to know where your sleeping quarters would be by the outside alone if someone were to try to assassinate you," I added, without thinking much about the intention.

However, his mouth turned into a coy smile. Even with that smile, his body tensed up slightly, prepared for anything. "Thinking about assassinating me, Wild?"

"Wouldn't serve me much good, would it? There are others who deserve my anger more than you do," I answered with a sigh. His body's tension relaxed ever so slightly.

"Good to know, Milana. Now, if you'll excuse me, I am late to a meeting with my second in command." He bowed his head before turning to walk away.

That was odd.

Behind me, Ivy cleared her throat and smiled mischievously when I glanced at her. Raising my eyebrow, I shook my head as the line went forward. No one else seemed surprised by his presence. In fact, it was like he never appeared at all. Like a ghost, with no one jumping out of his way or avoiding him.

"Well, well, well," she said, nudging my arm. "He certainly doesn't seem to mind you. I thought he'd avoid you after your arrival."

"Why's that?" I tilted my head as my mind grew suspicious, narrowing my eyes in response.

"It's not like you came into this Order willingly. Also, he's been gone hunting those down who were hunting *you*. Thor got on him about that. I wonder if he had any success. I hope so," Ivy said with a sigh as the line continued forward.

A chill rushed over my skin and through my veins. No one had ever tried hunting Desmond's men. No one ever bothered with a business that was not theirs. The world was a clear cut of the old saying my grandmother taught me, 'to each their own.' Women and children were protected, but only to a degree. A leader had to prioritize the masses over the singular person. Throwing me back out would have been much easier.

"Why would he do that?" I asked as my voice wavered in uncertainty.

"It's just how he is. Can't just leave well enough alone," Ivy added, a thin set of acid touching her words. Barely there if I didn't recognize it from my own speech patterns.

Every time my father told me to keep my head down and listen when Desmond took over, the bitterness I felt when my entire life turned upside down—the kind of bitterness laced with acid—never truly left me. Where Ivy's bitterness stemmed from was beyond me, and I didn't have it in me to ask.

Nodding to Ivy as she quickly adjusted her facial expression, I looked ahead. The entry to what could only be described as a massive communal center came into my view. My jaw slacked as I extended my neck for a better view.

Thousands of people were laughing and eating together, and there were still more behind me. Remembering the meals with those I loved flooded back, taking me off guard as I swallowed a lump in my throat. Some of the faces I saw I could have sworn I'd seen them before if I hadn't watched their executions years ago—faces I missed with all my heart. It would be no surprise they would find me when I was weak minded.

However, when one looked at me in the distance with just as much confusion in the far corners of the room, I blinked, and then the face was gone. Shaking my head, I continued forward.

"Everything okay?" Ivy asked, placing a hand on my shoulder.

"Just thought I saw someone," I said, shaking my head. "I'm fine."

"Wouldn't be surprising. There are some escapees from around the different Orders. In all your travels, it would be strange if you hadn't run into one of their faces." Ivy shrugged, and I couldn't help but wonder just how much she knew.

She comes across as an innocent, lacking common sense, and obtuse persona. However, the way her eyes glanced at me and to that particular group led me to believe that perhaps I underestimated her. Afterall, an underestimated woman could be a dangerous enemy or helpful ally, so long as I knew where we stood. She acted like we were allies, but I knew what it was like to play the game. I had to play it for years with Desmond until my escape. Feign stupidity and loyalty until I could run away.

Keeping this knowledge to myself for now, I simply nodded. "Perhaps."

The food line up was organized. Wooden plates were stacked high as we took one and moved to where the meal was. Piles of fresh fruit and vegetables, steaming fresh bread, and today it looked like a carved large bird for meat. Mead or juice was served in carved horn tankards, and I chose mead. The line moved quickly, and I waited for Ivy to finish her conversations with each of the women I was introduced five times over, and now that others were sitting, they took liberties to look at me.

I suppose it would be easy to see a new face in the crowd, and yet they only looked at me with curiosity and not the fear I was used to in other Orders.

Other Orders feared new people. They could disrupt the hierarchy if they challenged leaders to a fight and won. Either a Leader dying in a fight, or a formal challenge led to many uncertainties. Just the way many lived in an age of uncertainty. The destruction of society fifty years ago didn't give us much to go off of. Even then, my grandmother told me that humanity didn't change much at all. The fighting never stopped.

Ivy guided me to a spot near the center of the room. Benches and wooden tables lined wall to wall, leaving just enough room for a few people to pass comfortably. Even then, some left the room to eat in their own quarters. The amount of people made my skin crawl as my hearing and attentiveness went on high alert. Many talked around me and to me indirectly through Ivy. I would nod at most of her responses. Some of the questions I caught as I slowly ate were:

'Ah, this must be the one that came in with Thor, the one they had to knock unconscious?'

'Must be a Wild?'

'Is she wearing one of your creations?'

My brain started melding the words together as I finished my plate and looked around. I felt like a fish out of water, gasping for air, although no one seemed to notice. Being alone for so long—this was suffocating. I missed the silence, I missed the space, I missed many things.

"I have to go," I said as I stood up, not waiting for Ivy as I left my plate and ran from the room. My feet felt unsteady, but I tried to remember my way around to get outside. Fresh air was what I needed.

Panic was taking over and my body started heating up.

Not now…Escape. I need escape. I need to get away from here.

Just. Let. Me. Go.

In the panic, I could feel Desmond's cruel hands around my throat as my body tried to run faster. Knowing he could reach me from anywhere, Omar could be anywhere hunting for me under his orders. If they found me here and killed everyone as a message, it would be all my fault. What have I done? They always find me.

"Milana." A man's voice. Lyron's. I slowed down, but I didn't stop. I heard it again as I stumbled. That was all I remembered before my eyesight slowly blackened, the crash to the ground never hitting me. Just warm arms, cradling me.

LYRON

Going away for days on end, hunting in the unpredictable wilderness, was something I hadn't done in ages. I nearly forgot the thrill. I was hunting the men who tried to infiltrate my Order; the ones following Milana. Striving for peace for the last few years, keeping the border of our Order impeccably watched, and tending to the needs of my people before they become large issues were part of the day to day routine.

That. That I did for fun.

I was not a good man, just a man who wanted order in a world built on chaos. Most found that to be a rare trait, and my line of order was protection and stability. Two things scarce in our world. That meant I needed to be careful with who I let in my Order, and who I let run it with me. Thor was an easygoing, approachable man. Kira was a fierce woman, but maintained her composure. She was not entertained when I told her about Milana. The phrases out of her mouth were quite insulting. 'Arrogant idiot' was one of my favorites. But she wasn't wrong.

*****Three days ago*****

"You're going to accept another Wild? I can barely keep up the way it is, and she almost killed Oak! Are you stupid or just an arrogant idiot with a hero complex?" she yelled at me as she slammed her fists on the table. Her body frame was small, but she was strong. Most men didn't stand a chance in a fair fight. Hair short and light in color, it changed with the seasons, with how much she was outside helping with the crops.

"If you can't keep up, then step down," I said harshly, not caring for her attitude. "Plus, Thor vouched for her. Take it up with him."

"I'm so sick of men thinking with your lower heads. Honestly, it's pathetic. She's got a pretty face and you think she needs saving. How stupid are you?" Kira threw her hands up in exasperation.

I stood up and gave her a stare that made her stop in her tracks. My body was ready to strike, but control made me stay right where I was. Kira was a woman who knew how to take care of this Order. Never did I have to worry about the day to day functions outside of the ordinary. However, there was history.

"Another insult and you won't have to step down. I'll make you," I challenged. She lowered her head. "I know you mean well, but remember that I am still the Leader."

"For now," she said, lifting her head back up to meet my eyes with her light green ones. She had drive and determination that shined through them. I wouldn't doubt she'd make a good Leader. But I still had things to take care of that didn't allow me to step down *yet*.

"Yes, for now. Remember that when you meet her. Treat her well and keep your personal feelings aside. You are friends with Ivy and Thor vouched for her too," I said as she left the room, the door closing louder than usual. Smirking, I wondered what I did to have the privilege of so many strong-minded women in my life.

Finding the men's camp was easy. They weren't overly cautious as they traveled in a group of five. Killing them would be too easy. It solved a short-term problem without answers that I wanted. They had two on watch. One on each end of camp, neither of them even noticed I was there. I waited patiently, following them for two days before I finally heard what I wanted. Desmond wanted Milana.

Desmond.

That bastard had escaped me five years ago at the Mountain Order. I had heard of him through rumors and hearsay, but now I knew for sure. Milana was the key to killing him once and for all. These men would be back, and I was counting on it. For now, it seemed like they were heading to the Mountains west of us where they would receive further instructions from Desmond in the Desert Order. Going around Eagle Point Order would put them at a disadvantage, but finding that check point was vital to finally taking down Desmond's power run. Hearing what I had from those who had escaped him, he wanted revenge on me. However, his obsession with Milana set him over an edge once she ran from him.

I knew why, but it was a truth I didn't want to face yet.

Coming back home, it felt like an eternity had passed. Giving my intel to Thor was my priority, but seeing Milana in the line of people ready for their meal made me stop. She had a mind that thought on survival mode, constantly evaluating everyone and everything she saw. Challenging herself and others to exceed their limits, even if my patience was further challenged than anything when she was in her cell. Color had come back to her face, even if she was skeptical as she looked around. Before I knew it, I had to ask her what she thought of this place. To say I was surprised was an understatement.

"Omar is back with reinforcements," I told Thor once we were alone.

Punching the table Thor shook his head and sat down. "Determined bastard, isn't he?"

"Desmond is desperate. That much is certain. While there are those who escape, it wasn't as common until five years ago. While we take who we can, they always talk about how Desmond was obsessed with a Firan. Odd considering they are all men, right?"

"Yeah... I didn't remember him swinging that way either." Thor averted his gaze from me.

Odd.

"Unless there's a piece of the puzzle we are missing. Omar burned Ivy, which wouldn't make sense of they were looking for a Firan since Firans can't be burned by fire. However, I haven't had the pleasure of sitting down with one, so I guess I don't know," I said as I ran my fingers in my hair from my forehead to the top of my neck.

Thor's voice tightened. "Ivy has always avoided the issue. Every time she scampers away no matter how long its been. Some are like that but we would have so many more answers if she could tell us. I don't know what was all done to her, but Omar broke a piece of her." He always had a soft spot for Ivy, but Ivy never took him up on his advances. Now he considered himself a protector instead of a love interest.

I shook my head, a groan escaping me as I thought through the different scenarios.

Finally, I asked, "Thor, are any of them known Firans?"

"Um... what?" Thor hesitated.

"Are any of them known, Firans?" I repeated, annoyed, as I raised an eyebrow and mockingly slowed down my speech.

"A couple of them. Sorry, I thought you said... never mind," he said, clearing his throat. We went through descriptions of them, and he pointed out which ones he had confronted before.

"Everything okay?" I asked, narrowing my eyes. Not like him to completely blank out when talking about intel.

"Yeah, just had a lot going on since you wanted to play cat and mouse with the Desert boys. Surprised you just didn't wipe them out. Thought you'd be rusty," he said with a smirk.

"Not that rusty," I said, letting it go as we discussed the team to send out to follow them.

***

Coming back after my meeting with Thor, I saw her stumbling out in the hall, alone. That was not the same woman I saw just a short time ago. I caught up with her easily enough and grabbed her arm as she fell forward. Pulling her back towards me, she collided with my chest with a solid thud. She was burning up.

No wonder Thor was nervous the moment I brought the Firans into conversation.

Firans could not be affected by heat unless they lost control. Looking down at her, her chest heaved up and down from the labored breathing, her forehead scrunched. She looked to be in pain. Hauling her into my arms, I hooked an arm under her legs and under her upper back.

Not many were in the halls, but the ones that were certainly looked curious.

Damn it. Not what I wanted.

Instead of being smart and taking her to her room, I found myself at my own door. I prided myself on being calculating and effective, not a man to go with a moment. Opening the door, I sighed as it would allow me to keep an eye on her without her burning the whole place down.

Where she was a Firan who could control fire, I was an Airian. As much as I could fan the flames, I always knew how to snuff them out if needed.

CHAPTER FIVE — FIERY TRUTHS

LYRON

As my fingertips touched her arm, the heat seemed to pulse from her skin. A Firan was dangerous when their powers were not controlled. A woman Firan was unheard of, as far as I was aware. Of all the women, it made sense that Desmond hunted her. Desmond was obsessed with power. Milana could burn the world for him if he convinced her to. Some days I'd let him burn it all, but not this day, not with her.

Thor was chasing after the ones I found near our borders. Or at least sending someone to. I cared not which way that went. My time was to be spent here with this tricky Firan. Her hesitation to stay made sense, the desperation I saw when Thor talked to her in the woods, the way she flinched when we reached out for her. Everything slowly fell into place for me. Her fear was not of me, but of a former executioner of the Mountain Order. Desmond's quest for power did that.

Setting her down gently on a cushioned lounge chair, I touched her forehead, and I breathed a sigh of relief. Her temperature was not lowering, but it wasn't setting me on fire either. The relief came from more than this realization. However, that also meant more work for me. Change was brewing in the West, rumors were that Desert Order was losing their power grip on the people. Desmond would become desperate soon and come here himself since most of his men he sent after Milana kept dying. Not only by her hand—I had no problem killing them when they trespassed on my Order.

Desert Order Troops were followed by refugees that came in waves. Many stayed with us for a brief time before moving on. I wondered passively if any of them recognized Milana. Compassion was not an emotion that I had very often, but somehow this young woman with large caramel eyes, deep brown hair, and sun-kissed skin brought it out of me. Maybe I was losing my touch, maybe I was finally remembering what it felt like to feel human again. Either way, I needed to keep my edge if I was to take Desmond off guard. If he finds out she's here, he will want to burn not only this Order to the ground but see that I am destroyed.

He took everything from me. Returning the favor was the least I could do.

<u>MILANA</u>

I opened my eyes. The room was cased in orange from the lowering sun. Glancing around, I did not recognize where I was. The walls were round, but the room was large. A light blanket was draped over me as I turned to see Lyron glancing at the table in front of him, leaning over it as he stood. Standing up straight, he looked at me and his shoulders relaxed.

"I was worried when you had a temperature," he said, the pitch in his voice hitching slightly as I sat up. "I thought it may be stress related, but it faded fast. You should rest up. I can escort you back to your room if you'd like."

My brain raced as to why he would have brought me to what could very well be his private quarters. The more my eyes darted around the room, the more that seemed to be the case. A wave of panic swept through me as I realized I had no idea how long I was out for. I took a deep breath as I tried to keep my voice even, letting it out slowly as I gathered my raging thoughts.

"Why am I here?" I asked harshly.

"Didn't want you to burn your room down," he replied just as sharply, dropping the pretenses as much as I was. "I have an Order to take care of, and I never heard of a woman Firan."

"I should go," I muttered as I stood up.

The blood went to my head, and I stumbled. Lyron was in front of me to stop my fall as his hands touched my shoulders. He must have caught me before, too. I pulled away from him abruptly. If Lyron knew, then he knew why Desmond was after me. Firans were rare, even for the men in my Order. A Firan woman that Desmond could have at his disposal was what he had wanted in the best-case scenario. However, I was not a woman to be chained to burn the world down.

"You are free to go, if you wish," Lyron calmly stated.

He raised his shoulders, which then fell with each breath, ensuring my stability before stepping back two paces to give me some space. Confused by his words, I tilted my head. This was the perfect opportunity to go. I should run out of the door with a smile on my face, and yet I felt a pull to hear him out.

"But..." I prompted him, presuming there was a continuation.

He smirked, shaking his head. "But I would like to offer you a deal. Stay here for my protection. If you stay, I will make sure Desmond never touches you again."

"What's in it for you?" I asked as I narrowed my eyes.

"The guarantee that Desmond will come. I have a score to settle. I want you to stay as bait. He's desperate to find you, to take you back, to do whatever twisted version of ownership he has to you. I want to protect you from him while seeing the life drain from his eyes by my hand," he offered, his eyes growing darker with every word.

He meant every word, and they sent chills down my spine. When Thor offered protection, it was for solely a hero's purpose. Lyron wanted something more—revenge.

"If I say 'no'?"

"Then I'm simply back to square one and I'll try to lure the bastard another way," he said with a slight shrug. I didn't sense hostility or ill intent. Lyron was direct, but his voice was even and clear. "But I am currently sending Thor out on a mission to capture some men I found in my patrol the last few days. I believe you may know him, but it may take time for him to come back depending on intel. If you wish to stay until then, I will not object."

"You want to use me as bait, but keep me safe?" I said, clarifying his general idea. "There may be a prisoner coming from the Desert Order and you want me to stay because..."

"Because I want you to tell me just how much he could know based on your previous knowledge. You have knowledge that none of us have on the inner workings of Desmond's Order. Many refugees refuse to talk, but you have been hunted by Desmond. That wasn't just a passing phase. He's obsessed."

"Obviously, he's insane," I said, raising my hands in frustration. I brought them down by my hips with a clapping sound. Taking a deep breath, I glanced at Lyron, who nodded in agreement. "How do you know him? Why do you want revenge?"

"I knew him a long time ago. We were both assigned to deal with undesirables in the Mountain Order. I have my reasons for wanting to kill him," he assured me, turning back to his table. That was the end of that discussion.

He pointed to his table and cocked his head for me to come over. As I did, he cleared his throat. Papers were laid out, and I realized it was a timeline. '

Litha 43 AC – Desmond joined Mountain Order.

Ostara 45 AC – Desmond accepts Judge position.

Hallows 45 AC – Desmond starts Executions.

Mabon 46 AC – Desmond is exiled from Mountain Order. Heads West to Desert.

There were records in between of specific accounts of his dealings for each listing, but it was obvious he caused chaos for three years in the Mountain Order and the Desert Order.

"I gathered his information after what happened at the Mountain Order. He killed whoever defied him, and whatever denied him. The Mountain Leader, Tibs, enjoyed Desmond's drive and passion for order. When he created a position unique to Desmond, as Tibs had a second and third already, Desmond took that inch and nearly destroyed the Order. He has no end game, just domination," Lyron said before sighing. "Think about the offer. I'll bring you back to your room."

I nodded. I was not mad at being bait because he was honest with me. He didn't want to be my hero—he had an objective. But I didn't want to *watch* Desmond die. I wanted to be the *reason* he begged for his life. Walking through the halls, that thought lingered. Innocent Milana died a long time ago, but what rose from the grave was me. Broken and bruised, but still breathing and willing to do what was necessary to keep what little peace I had.

As Lyron stopped in front of my room, I grabbed his forearm as he turned to leave. "I'm not in need of saving. I want to be the reason he drops to his knees, begging to be saved. I want to watch the life burn out of his eyes as he dies slowly in agony. He destroyed my life. I will not just be bait. I will not stand by and watch you take your revenge. Keep that in mind if I decide to stay." I let go of his arm.

I was satisfied when his eyes widened as I shut my door. Lyron and I had the same agenda, and I wanted us to be on the same level. A smile formed on my lips. Perhaps I had a good reason to stay after all.

***

The next morning, there was an incessant knocking on my door. Groaning, I nearly fell out of bed as I rolled to get up. Straightening, I mumbled about it being too early. While I'd slept well last night—too well—my body felt like it could sleep for days. Yawning, I stretched my arms up to get some blood flowing.

"Who is it?" I asked, rubbing the sleep out of my eyes.

"If you don't open this door, I will find a way in there," Ivy proclaimed, her voice shrill and absolute. I grinned and shook my head.

I unlocked my door and waved her inside. She looked at me in shock before holding up an apple, one I took a little too willingly.

"You look well rested," she said, narrowing her eyes as she glanced around the room. "Alone?"

"Why would I have company?" I bit into the sweet apple.

"Oh, honestly, I wonder," she said, as if it was a joke.

When I shrugged, her eyes almost bugged out of her head. "People saw you with Lyron, tan skin, platinum blonde hair. Maybe you know him?"

"Hard to miss him. What does that have to do with me being alone in my room?" I knew full well what she was asking, but watching her hackles rise with the lack of information was entertaining.

"Are you bedding each other?" she asked with more forwardness than I gave her credit for.

I almost spit out the apple. "What would give you that idea?" I contended after I made sure I could breathe right.

"Well, people saw Lyron carrying you," she began, her brow furrowing with worry. She approached my table, leaning in slightly as she continued. "What happened to you yesterday? You bolted like a trapped rabbit during mealtime."

"I'm not used to so many people and I panicked. I felt trapped, and I lost it. Lyron found me when I was fainting and then I woke up and we talked. He escorted me back here, and that was it. No 'bedding,'" I finished, trying to hold back a chuckle.

"Still, I'd be careful. A lot of women aren't too happy," she warned as she took a bite out of her own apple.

"Why is that? Oh wait, let me guess, he's desired by *all the women* and now they are after me?" I hoped she was exaggerating.

From her nod, I groaned and laid down on my bed and shook my head before taking another bite. We ate in silence before she finished, setting her core down on the table. Pushing herself off the table, she sat at the foot of my bed.

"The ladies here are tight-knit. He's everyone's fantasy. No one could get at him, so he was safe to admire. If he's admiring you, the fantasy is done and you are the common enemy, but if you're not interested, then maybe it won't be so bad," she said, trying to reason it all out for me.

"But he's a real person, not a fantasy. Seems weird so many would be that unrealistic. It's hard enough to get by day to day. If people hate me for a reason so childish, then so be it. I am not here to make friends. I didn't even want to be here." I yelled the last part, making Ivy flinch. "I'm sorry, I got carried away."

Ivy stood up, her eyes blinking, and her breathing measured. "I know you didn't ask to be here," she said in a calm, quiet tone, "but I think you should experience the hot springs before you decide to go. Would you like to? They're nice in the cool mornings like today."

"Will I be ambushed by a hoard of angry, love-sick women?" I asked, smirking.

"Well, if you are, at least you'll be bathed," Ivy giggled and I laughed.

Making our way to the hot springs was easy enough. Through the front arch, there was a stone path. Only minimal glares followed me as Ivy led me down the winding path to the evergreens and into their dense shade. A round pool of steaming water could be found not too far inside the cave. Although the cave was empty, its well-used path and stones outside showed signs of frequent use.

Undressing, I put my clothes aside with care and kept alert as Ivy gave a loud, relaxed sigh. Ivy had thrown her clothes on the ground and stepped in so fast you'd think she was deprived of the experience.

"Relax, it's guarded," she reassured, waving her hand.

That only made me tense up, but she leaned her head back and practically melted in the water. So carefree.

I was jealous.

I tilted my head back, submerging my scalp but not my face. Scratching at my scalp, I cleaned up as Ivy soaked. We stayed quiet. The only sounds were my movements in the water and distant bird songs. As the quiet dragged on, I relaxed more. In my own way, but not as much as Ivy. I massaged my shoulders and calves as both were incredibly tense.

I finally cleared my throat. "Should we head back?"

"Are you going to stay?" Ivy asked quietly.

I didn't answer. I had none to give. Being saved was not my intention, but being hunted forever wasn't either. Lyron offered a middle ground, but that only offered my revenge, not the full satisfaction of it.

"If you're leaving, do it soon," she said as she got out of the water.

Seeing her burn scars brought it all back. The nightmares, the screams in my dreams, as I remembered every person who Desmond had tortured and burned. Since I was immune to fire, I had to watch or risk being exposed. I wanted Desmond to *suffer*.

As I dressed, I followed Ivy, who suggested taking my meal to my room until I got used to people. At the entry arch way, I told her I had something to do. She let me part and I quickly headed to Lyron's room.

I heard him muttering behind the door as I knocked insistently, despite his belief that one knock was sufficient. He opened the door and his eyes widened, clearly surprised to see me.

"How did Ivy get those burns?" I demanded.

"I think you know," he said, moving aside to let me in. He shut the door behind me and folded his arms.

"Yes, I do, but not the details. Do you know who did it?"

"The one Thor is tracking down," he answered, narrowing his eyes.

"What?"

"Hot springs?" he asked, pointing to my wet hair. "Quite forward of you coming to my room after a bath? You know customs, right?"

I thought about it before my eyes widened. Before a man and woman were officially together, they would bathe. I pursed my lips, not knowing what to say. My face heated. "I hadn't thought about it. What I thought about is how you have a good grasp on Desmond's movements and his lackeys. So, I will stay, but I will not stay to be saved. I will make sure he suffers at my hand. You have your reasons and I have mine. I will only stay if you see me as an equal in this vendetta. I want to know everything you know, but for now, I will find something better to do than linger in your room. Apparently, the women are already upset with me after seeing us together. Can't fight the entire Order," I said, making my way for the door.

He chuckled, "I'm sure you'll find a way," as I ran down the hall embarrassed.

Idiot.

<u>DESMOND</u>

Five years and still that little mouse runs from me. Her parents had given her to me willingly, and even as I slit their throats, she had the nerve to run. My blade should have struck her as I threw it into the crowd that day, but a meddlesome old woman took the fatal blow. My calculations were precise: get the girl, use her powers, and rule the Desert Order with an iron fist. Then expand my rule to the Mountain Order, Earth Order, and finally the Eagle Point Order.

Lyron took my pet mouse and made her his own. That would not do.

As the paper crinkled in my grasp, I let out an exasperated sigh. If I wanted anything done right, I had to do it myself. However, this little rebellion that started after *she* left has been irritating. Once I think I killed the head of the snake, another would emerge even more annoying than the last.

Standing before the double doors to my veranda, I watched people walked by, darting glances as they quickened their pace. The world was complacent due to fear, not respect. I was well versed in the immersion of fear. Lyron had troubles with my methods in the Mountain Order. He still wanted to take what was mine, even after eight years. He just couldn't keep his grubby hands to himself. I suppose chopping them off could help.

I smirked. The thought of him bleeding out on the floor as I took back my mouse gave me hope. A word I despised. A word that meant nothing in the grand scheme of things. I didn't want her to hope. I wanted her to grovel, obey and submit to her fate as my goddess of death and *me* as her god.

My eyes closed as I envisioned her long brown hair braided to the side, her sheepish, golden-brown eyes as she avoided direct eye contact with me, and the way she moved was purposeful and elegant and somehow completely awkward. Perfection in the ways of meek and obedient.

When she spat in my face and ran full force into the desert, I admit I was stunned. Many of my men died that day. They failed me, and that led to an uprising. At least it gave me something to do. I enjoyed killing, but I was not a Firan. The destruction I caused was embarrassingly weak compared to burning another. Despite her meek little form, she had the ability to cause agony and destruction. The irony was too much.

And then she kept escaping my best hunters. Whatever snapped in her unleashed the fury I had been waiting for. My obsession was far from healthy. I knew that. Patience was not a virtue I planned on developing either. The time was coming for me to go hunt her down myself. To demand her obedience and see that she bowed before me.

Yes, my mouse. Soon, I'll be coming.

CHAPTER SIX — ENVIOUS REFLECTIONS

<u>Milana</u>

Avoiding Lyron was impossible. I gave up trying after the last two days of constantly running into him. With Thor leading the small operation to capture Desmond's men, he'd been missing from my day-to-day life. Kind of miss the energetic personality. Instead, I had Lyron—the man on a mission. While we established our agreement, he'd been popping up everywhere. Truly, I missed my nomad life of the solitaire quiet in the forest.

I sighed heavily, feeling a presence behind me. Turning around slowly, I raised my eyebrow and put my hand on my hips. "You know this is harassment, right?" I groan.

"Hardly," he countered and walked ahead of me. "Now you're following me. We happen to be going to the same area. It's a lovely day, is it not?"

"Uh huh," I said, shaking my head as I walked behind him.

The sunny day was perfect for a trip to the lake, and it was still early enough that most people wouldn't be up yet. Of course, Lyron *would be awake* and going to the lake as well. Narrowing my eyes, I glared at the back of his head, willing him to turn off before we made it to the path of flattened grass and pressed dirt that headed straight to the lake. I couldn't will this man to go anywhere else because he was heading dead straight to my destination.

"So, I guess even leaders need some lake time?" I asked.

"I suppose so. I find the water soothing when I have to think," he said.

"Ah, well, don't let me distract you. I can go somewhere else," I offered, ready to turn around.

"No, your presence will be pleasant. I find you refreshing. Are you planning on swimming?" he asked, tilting his head so he could see me in his peripheral.

"Not fully. Just dipping my feet in will help. The heat doesn't bother me much," I said, alluding to my Firan abilities. I only felt uncomfortable when my abilities were out of control. However, a sunny day like this was pleasant. "What do you mean, you find me refreshing?"

He took a moment before he stopped. Turning around, he smiled gently. A sight I didn't see, as his expressions were usually stoic and direct. Out of all the leaders I met in my travels, he was an odd one. He didn't seek power, but he embraced it all the same. His stature was towering, his demeanor authoritative, but the way he had control was out of respect and care instead of oppression and demands.

"You're honest. You do as you want, regardless of my desire to protect you. You do not wish to impress me, you mostly want me to leave you alone. People in my position find that rare, and I find myself isolated. Your frustration at having me around makes me selfishly amused," he said before stifling back a brief laugh.

My mouth opened slightly to say something, but closed just as quickly. So, I reacted how I did to most compliments. Deflection. "Glad I amuse you, but I want to reach the lake sometime today." After urging him a few steps, he laughed and walked with more energy. *Smug brat*, I thought with a smile.

As we reached the lake, he slipped off his footwear. He looked lost in thought, so I sat further inland to give him space. I didn't think of the duties of a leader, but knew most weren't worthy of it. Lyron was different. As much as I groaned when I saw him and he popped up wherever I was, I couldn't say that I hated it completely. While my presence was refreshing to him, I found him agreeable. Thor acted like he wanted to save me. Lyron was comfortable letting me decide for myself. That could have been one of the few reasons I decided to stay at Eagle Point Order.

Laying on my back in the grass, I closed my eyes and let my mind wander as I soaked up the sun's rays. The rhythmic lapping of the water against the shore was lulling me to sleep before the sun was blocked. Opening my eyes, Lyron was above me, hinged forward by his hips, and his white hair fell forward, nearly brushing my face from his braid.

I sighed and frowned. "You're blocking the sun," I noted, sitting up as he straightened.

"I had something on my mind, and you didn't answer when I called." He sat down next to me. "There's a festival we hold every year for those who wish to challenge for leadership. Kira, Thor, and I will all be under pressure if there are challengers. Not that I'm particularly worried about it. I just don't want you to feel it's like other Orders. Other orders are brutal, as you know. Here, we celebrate strength and those who lack it. I wanted this event to be peaceful when it began. Sometimes outside challengers come in, but it's also a test of strength if you'd rather not fight for leadership and challenge a worthy opponent. I came here today to hope for another good year. You are welcome to participate if you want to test your battle skills."

"Interesting. So, the challenges are welcomed here? I never heard of such a thing. Most people dread the challenges or changes, but then most have it worse off than here. While most Orders have rough leadership, people get used to it. "It can be overwhelming for constant change and stress," I said, trailing off.

"Coming from experience?" Lyron asked, and I nodded.

Desmond destroyed my faith in the challenges. Maybe that's why Lyron informed me in advance. Knowing I'm a Firan and knowing Desmond, it wouldn't be shocking he thought of this ahead of time. Thoughtfulness was an oddity in today's world, but I appreciated it.

Taking off my footwear, I stood up and made my way to the water. The cool, clear water lapped at my ankles as I dug my toes in the colder sand below the surface. The tiny granules of sand massaged my feet gently as I curled and flexed my toes. Stretching my arms above me, I turned; Lyron who was watching beyond me with intent. He looked at me with a tense smile.

As I wondered what was bothering him, I put it in my mind that it was truly not my place to solve his problems. Maybe *I* had the savior issue.

<u>Lyron</u>

An uneasiness spread through me as I received Thor's brief report our hawk had relayed through a small piece of paper tied to its leg. Thor personally went with three of our best trackers; two were killed by Desmond's men.

However, the job was done.

Going to the lake was a habit of mine when I lost good people. I remembered them as the light of the sun glittered across the surface. I prioritized being strong for my people, yet allowed myself a moment to grieve. Usually, I had the space to myself, but today was a surprise. Today, there was Milana.

"Earlier, you inquired about Ivy," I said, turning to face her.

"You told me it was not your story to tell," she replied, raising an eyebrow.

"I did. However, you know as I do how Desmond works. The burns on her body were from his hunt for you. That doesn't make it your fault…"

"Doesn't it though?"

"No, that doesn't make it your fault. He targeted Wild women, assuming you'd avoid men. At first, I didn't understand why, but when Thor brought her back, she said nothing of it. She didn't speak to me about that time. Thor only told me what he saw. Then you came, and even you hardly speak of his crimes. I realize they are legion, but I can only explain so much about him. We both know how dark and twisted he is. Never forget you are not the only one who he wronged, but we can end the nightmare from continuing," I offered as best I could for her to trust me.

Milana was a fierce soul. Her drive to survive and persevere made me remember when I was a Wild after leaving the Mountain Order. Every action counted when surviving on your own. Thor made an alliance with me soon after and we developed a place for outcasts to feel welcomed. Outcasts like Kira, Ivy, Oak, and so many others deserved a place to be safe. I could provide that for them, but Milana did not want protection. She wanted to thrive on her own terms. I respected her for that choice and want her to feel understood. Mentally and physically.

Her smirk had disappeared and was replaced by a sympathetic smile. *Was she comforting me?* I did not deserve comfort. What I deserved was a slow death for all the sins I committed, but the world did not work in fairness. Fairness is an illusion brought upon by those who could not stomach reality. Life was unpredictable. Strength ensures survival, but children grow up regardless, just like warriors perish.

"You're right," she said after a moment of calm silence. "He did wrong many people. But he made a severe mistake, he wronged us."

I felt the grin form on my face as she stood up straighter. Her demeanor changed in that moment. Confidence radiated from her, as if she finally understood she had an ally and a purpose that was set out.

"Yes," I responded. "You're very right, Milana."

Milana

After heading back to my room, I thought of Lyron's words. Did he genuinely think of me as an equal? Someone to rely on? His words lit a fire in me I thought was extinguished.

Hope.

My small existence was driven by survival and fear for so many years that I forgot the strength I had. I was a Firan. Powerful and strong, able to burn the world down if I wished. Passionate and driven. Never forgetting those who helped me and those who wronged me. I realized that I had forgotten how to live my life and not just survive. I could have my revenge and help others stay safe. While I lived my life for me out of necessity, Lyron offered me time and resources to plan and orchestrate what I wanted for so long. And he offered it as my ally.

While my days were spent helping Ivy with clothing and wandering the compound, I had to admit my days were boring. I wanted excitement and to hone my skills. Something other than the day-to-day grind. I wanted to train to become a stronger person, stronger warrior. To show Thor that I didn't need to be protected. That I could protect them.

My thoughts were heard as a clank of metal sounded in the distance while I explored a new part of the fortress.

The fortress was simple once the pattern was realized. There were three wings from the main entry point that formed halls into larger rooms, mess halls mostly, but they could be used for other gatherings as well. Rooms from the main wings formed a square, providing a view of the mess hall from above.

"Welcome to the fight pit." I heard Lyron's voice behind me.

My shoulders jolted slightly as I whipped around. Taking a deep breath, I shook my head. "Ah, holding out on me."

"Not really. I knew you'd find it eventually," he said. "Thor comes back tomorrow with our prisoners."

"Oh goodie, another one of you to find me no matter how much I try to avoid you," I said as I rolled my eyes.

Being used to it was one thing, dealing with it was another.

"I thought you enjoyed my company," Lyron said, furrowing his brows as he frowned.

"Sometimes, but others not as much. Hardly necessary to follow me to every meal after one moment of panic," I replied, raising my eyebrow.

"But it was panic, and I worry. It's good that you found this place. I would be interested in sparing with you," he said.

"Sparring?" I questioned, narrowing my eyes, wondering if he was truly serious.

"Yes, I want to see what your basics are besides throwing your head into someone's nose," he said, smirking.

Confidence radiated from him as he folded his arms and waited for my response. But he already knew it.

"If necessary, I'd fight dirty again. Honor only gets you so far." I shrugged.

"I won't say you're wrong, but there are fundamentals I think you're missing," he said, laughing as the two men practicing sword skills turned with eyes wide. "Come with me, we can use wooden swords."

"Wooden swords? Why would you use a wooden sword?" In what battle a wooden sword would be helpful besides battering someone repeatedly?

"It's to prevent harm to the other person. I don't know your skills as you do not know mine. This makes sure that harm is not caused, unless if you'd rather we use actual swords and test fate?" He grabbed the wooden sword anyway and handed it to me.

With a roll of my eyes, I grabbed it and we found space away from the real blade wielders. It's a safe way to gauge my abilities against someone trained in battle. I steadied myself as I swung the sword to measure how it felt in my hands.

"Your wrist is bending too much, too flimsy. Keep it strong and steady. The blade is an extension of your arm," he corrected as he demonstrated the difference in moving his wrist versus keeping it steady. "Much more power behind a swing when you're using your arm and body to swing rather than just moving your wrist about. Easiest way to break it."

He corrected my stance, my hold, my footing, and other intricate details I had never considered. I was never trained formally, so this was eye opening. I was smiling by the time Kira came into view. She looked puzzled as she looked between Lyron and me.

"I came to let you know Thor sent a message. One prisoner took their own life, so they only have one. Apparently, they paint a pretty picture of being captured by you. You're spending your time elsewhere," she said, scanning me before looking back at Lyron.

"Do you have a problem with me?" I asked sternly.

"I have a problem with Lyron not performing his duties as Leader because you are taking up his time." Kira raised her eyebrows. "Don't flatter yourself thinking I have time to have a personal problem with you."

"Kira," Lyron's voice lowered in warning.

"No, you have been following her like a lost pet. You have an Order to run, not just make sure one is fine. Refugees are coming in more frequently and yet I don't see you giving them lessons on swordsmanship. You have a job to do, so do it," Kira yelled. She left without giving Lyron a chance to respond.

Silence stretched between us. An awkward moment that lasted an eternity. Kira's behavior towards me was not the usual stern attitude as Ivy had described her.

"I apologize for Kira. She's stressed but I will talk with her later," Lyron said, running his hand through his hair.

"Don't apologize for her. Let her feel as she does. When you have time, can you continue helping me? I don't want you to stop being a good leader just so show me how to fight. You have an event coming up," I said, brushing off her words for now. Come the event, I would challenge her. Screw her.

<u>Lyron</u>

Kira had been one of my most fiercely loyal followers, so much so that you couldn't quite call her a friend, although for a time she admitted feelings for me. One tradition I did not take part in was procreating. I planned to dedicate my life to researching the time before the Calamity and never have kids. In retrospect, I could see that night was harsh for many reasons.

Kira came to me a year ago. Her hair was longer then, braided, and she smelled of flowers when she opened the door to my quarters. The faint smell wafting in as she closed the door gently behind her. I found it odd given she wasn't timid.

The bonding festival was in full swing by the sounds of the drums and laughter outside below my window, and I was confused why she sought me out in my quarters. I was famously distant at this tradition, and I made it a point to keep it that way.

Her fingers twisted with each other, and her knuckles were white, face flushed, and breathing shallow. I worried she was sick, so I stood up and walked towards her from my desk.

"You can stay there. What I have to say is already embarrassing," she exhaled as I sat back down.

"Are you unwell? You seem out of sorts," I said as I narrowed my gaze at her. She was the third in command. I wanted to ensure her health for the upcoming chaos of couples learning their coupling results. With her overseeing the in-house tasks, Thor oversaw reconnaissance, and I was to delegate everything else that didn't fall in those categories and even helping them with those issues. I needed her to be at her healthiest. I was not emotionally equipped to deal with hormonal women in droves.

"I'm fine. I just got to spit it out. I would like to join with you Lyron, for a child. There I said it," she pushed her hands out to her sides and shook them. Ridding herself of the burden.

I stood up, hitting my knee on the desk, and froze. My eyes wide, she looked at me expectantly, nodding her head for me to respond. Her patience was never part of her personality.

"Say something, please, Lyron," she said, looking around frantically to avoid my gaze that studied her. She spoke frantically, saying she wanted a child and didn't know who to ask because she knew I wasn't looking for anyone. Anyone else would have jumped on the opportunity, and she picked the one man that couldn't give her what she wanted.

I held my hand up and she stopped talking immediately. My head pounded as the calculations ran through my head of not wanting her to leave being my third in command, but not wanting what she wanted was even crueler if we did have a child.

"Kira, I'm sorry," I whispered before clearing my throat. "I am truly sorry, but I am not the man for this. I do not want children, and to pretend to want what you want is not fair to you. Please, find someone else. The festival is still young. Please don't cry."

Her eyes started welling up with tears and she took her wrist and harshly rubbed her cheeks where the tears fell. "Fine. Thank you for being honest," she said with a sniffle before she smiled. "At least I know I won't be the only one refused by you. Honestly, you're too good looking for your own good. That will be the last time you hear me say it. I just got caught up in my own mind. Sorry to bother you."

And she was gone. She vanished like a spirit, leaving only a sweet floral scent behind. Bittersweet reminder of what a broken man I was.

Although I spoke the truth, she avoided me for a while. Other women did too. Somehow it led to much less awkward confrontations, as to how Kira made that message known was beyond me. The inner workings of women networking scared me enough as it was. They surpassed the abilities of highly trained spies. Despite being argumentative, Kira efficiently managed the Order's daily operations and food storage. Her pride in her work was astounding, and it showed in the trust the others had in her. Not everyone liked her, but most learned to respect her. I was unsure whether to intervene or ignore her response to Milana. Dealing with women was not my specialty.

I came back to the present as Milana looked at me with a fierce gaze. My own eyes widened and even my cheeks flushed warmly. little Firan was keeping me on edge and yet her presence comforted me.

"Yes?" I asked as she continued to stare at me.

"I want to challenge her," Milana said, and it nearly made me lose my balance.

Massaging my temple, I shook my head. "That would be ill advised," I said with a small groan.

"Why? You said the festival could lead to anyone challenging, so why not? I want to punch that smug attitude right off her face." She punched one hand into the other. Her courage and determination were astounding. Almost as much as her stubbornness and lack of reading a room.

"I did say that, but I would advise not to go against Kira. You are new to the Order and if you intend to stay, may I suggest not making waves out of a slight issue," I said, walking up to Milana to take her wooden sword. Obviously, training was done for today. She thrust the sword into my extended hand and pursed her lips together.

"Small issue?" Milana drew out each word as if it was the worst thing to come out of my mouth. Judging by the breath she was taking in, I was about to learn exactly how she felt about it. "Kira just openly said you were neglecting your job, and that I was a problem. She hasn't even been around to welcome me. As you say, her job is to take care of the Order internally. Some bullshit job she's doing. I don't expect her to wait on me, but if she wants to talk about someone not doing their job, then she is not doing her part either. I'm not one to take crap like that lying down and cry about it. If she has a problem with me and can't talk to me, then I'll confront them and make sure they understand exactly where I expect the respect to be drawn. I don't care about taking her spot as a third in command. Screw that. I just want to punch her face and see the look as she falls to the ground."

This woman was going to be the death of me.

"Kira hardly earned her a spot by allowing someone to punch her in the face. But I'm done with this conversation. Do whatever you wish. This is between the two of you," I said, taking our training swords to the wall where I hung them back up.

She uttered "fine" before I turned around. Where'd she go? I could hear her grumbling out of the arena, though. I looked up and saw Oak, whom Milana had knocked out with her dagger's hilt.

"She's a fiery one," he commented, just barely loud enough for me to hear.

"You have no idea." Luckily, he didn't get my meaning as he cocked his head to the side. "Never mind. Are you done resting?"

He barked a laugh and smiled broadly. "I can't stand staying in bed. Sunny may kill me though. It's been too long since I got to stretch my legs. Plus, one of the guys told me that you were training the one who knocked my lights out. I'm just glad it was before you trained her and not after. Thor will be surprised when he gets back. Took a liking to her, that one did."

While it didn't surprise me, it didn't change the fact that it left a sour taste in my mouth. "Huh? Did he now?"

"You know him. He likes the lost causes."

CHAPTER SEVEN — FESTIVAL

<u>Milana</u>

My blood boiled as I stomped through the halls to get outside. My anger towards Kira increased with each thought. Her words wrapped around my anger, growing until it wanted to explode. As my breathing grew shallow, I felt my control slipping again. Being around people was bad for me. I never lost control this much in the years I've been by myself. Closing my eyes, I took deep breaths, slowly drawing energy from the ground and letting my anger subside enough to not feel as if I was going to burn her face off.

Looking outside, I realized I walked past the market and sat on the outskirts just out of sight of the front archway. The grass was tall around me as I sat down and stretched out my legs. Trees before me lined the forest as I heard the bird chirping within them. For once, I had a moment of peace. I heard a twig snap and quickly turned around.

"Bad day, eh?" Tucker said from behind me as my shoulders jolted in surprise.

I smirked and said, "Kira doesn't like me much."

"I can see that. Lyron likes ya, so does Thor. She's been trying to get Lyron's attention for ages. When he told her she wasn't what he wanted, she hated everyone who even caught a glance from him. She calmed down until you showed up. Now she's all flustered again," he said, shaking his head. "Young love is a weird thing."

"Love, ha," I scoffed at the idea of it. Love was hardly part of my vocabulary and anyone who claimed to love someone usually only lusted after them.

"Yeah, it's there. Messy and unpredictable, but love none the less. Sometimes it looks like lust, sometimes obsession, but it all stems from the idea of being with someone. I loved a woman once. We had a couple of children, but the world is cruel. They were all taken from me many years ago. Poisoned by the air, she was from before the Calamity too and never adjusted like I did. Hurt to breathe for years, but the boys were taken when there was a fight in the Order we lived in. Got caught in the middle of it, thought they'd make a stand as young men fighting for a fool of a Leader," he said as his eyes gazed out into the distance into the forest, his mind a million memories away.

"My parents gave me up to marry the leader of my old Order. The Leader killed them both. My brother died fighting to rebel. Anyone who I cared for has left me or betrayed me. Love is not part of my life. It's a joke," I said bitterly as I looked to the ground.

"Maybe so, but to some, it's the only thing they hold onto. Like you and that anger," he said piercing a bit too deep with that accusation. "You keep that anger like it defines you, but you are much more than that. I haven't talked to you much, but I know you are more than that anger you keep inside you. Too much anger burns away at your soul until there's nothing left. Revenge slowly chips away at your sanity. If you want revenge, don't take it to get back at the person. Find justice for those he wronged, including yourself. This former Leader of yours doesn't deserve to have space in your mind anymore than you need him in your life. Keeping that idea is like a cancer. No one heals from if you don't cut it out. I told my sons this and I'll tell you. Don't hold on to anger and hate, it only ends up killing pieces of you until there's nothing left. Then when you act on that revenge from the hate, when you pierce that bastard through the heart, nothing will be solved."

I looked at Tucker in awe, my mouth gapping, and eyes wide as he put his hand on my shoulder and patted it twice. I heard his words, but my mind rebelled against it. Revenge has always been on my mind, hatred for Desmond was always there. I can't forgive him, but Tucker said nothing about forgiveness.

"I'll leave ya to your thoughts, but just remember what I said," he said, walking away after he winked at me.

"What if he deserves death?" I asked desperately.

"I never said to forgive him, just find a different reason than revenge to kill the bastard. Justice for those he did wrong to, remember?" he said as he continued to walk away.

Justice, not revenge. The thought was new to me. He wronged so many friends and my family. People I grew up with... and even Lyron. Ivy. Desmond's reach knew no bounds but justice instead of revenge. The thought made me even more mad, but also there was a pain in my chest. As if my heart was going to be ripped out if I put aside the thought for justice. I wished he would die for what he did, but realizing how many others he hurt caused pain in my chest.

Ivy didn't deserve what happened to her from his orders. While he could not burn her since he was not a Firan, I could imagine his order gave the way to that horrific act. Her torture would have been painful, her nerves slowly dying off one by one as it felt searing hot to ice cold. The nerves not knowing how to process the information of being burned, people have said it feels ice cold after so much heat. The only way you're aware of the burning is the smell. The stench of burning flesh was one that no one forgot.

Shaking my head of the thought of her torture, I felt tears welling up past my lashes. Rubbing my cheeks to dispel them, I felt shame. Shame for being unable to take my revenge sooner, failing to save her from that fate.

"Hey, you," I heard Ivy behind me as I tried to stop the tears. She could not see my face yet. Nor did I want her to. "You okay?"

I shook my head but remained silent.

"You know you can talk to me right," Ivy said as she touched my shoulder. "I know Kira comes across as rash, but she's a good person. She just hates how you got to Lyron, and he doesn't mind you either."

Damn her for being too considerate. Kira was a million thoughts away by now and a small, choked laugh escaped me as I realized that's why she thought I was crying. The news of Kira yelling at me and Lyron seems to have spread rapidly, but I've moved on from it.

Looking at her, I shook my head. While she wouldn't understand my meaning, I quietly said, "I'm so sorry."

"Hey, don't worry about Kira, get inside so we can eat because I am hungry," she said as she stepped in front of me and grabbed my hands that were hugging my knees. "Tell me all about training with Lyron? Are you sure you guys aren't a thing?"

I laughed as she pulled me up and pushed for me to walk inside. "No, we aren't a thing." I told her about the training and everything leading up to Kira, and she listened and smiled. Revenge slipped my mind for a moment.

***

The next day, I heard the craze around the Order that Thor had returned. He returned unharmed and the young ladies were thrilled. A couple of small cuts on his arm, but they say the scars would add to his charm. I would roll my eyes as they talked. I hadn't seen him or the prisoner yet. Not that I expected to, but just seeing the confirmation would have been nice since I have no idea where they'd kept me locked away. I was always curious where they had kept me, but they must have taken me around a couple of different spots because retracing my steps never worked.

I was surprised that I hadn't seen Thor yet since he was so determined to keep me in his sights before he left. Lyron and Ivy hadn't approached me yet, either. Odd. Taking this rare moment of quiet, I escaped to the hot springs down the rock steps at the bottom of the hill. I gathered a towel and clothes, listening for anyone nearby. Quiet surrounded me and I felt my steps hurrying with joy as a smile spread across my face.

I could hardly remember a time since I came here that I was alone outside. Someone always monitoring me was not enjoyable when I was used to my solitude. Nature was my escape, and the sounds of the birds and the fresh air were a form a solace. The fact they protected this land too from dangers was hard to get used to, but I let my guard down from time to time now to just enjoy myself. Something I hadn't done in years.

I plopped myself in the hot springs and looked around one last time. No one around. I took my hands and spread them over the top of the water. Concentrating, I transferred heat from my hands to the water. The problem with being a Firan was that heat affected me different, I almost needed to be scorched to feel any effects. I hoped no one needed a bath for a while.

Feeling my muscles relax, I leaned my head back and felt my joints pop and loosen as I stretched. My arms went above my head and I felt like I was being watched. While I wasn't exposed fully, there wasn't much for coverage here.

After a few moments of peace, I felt it. Eyes were watching me. I could feel the weight of them as my neck tensed up again. Seeing a quick shake of a bush, I sighed. No threat here.

"Come out, creeper," I said, tilting my head, and I saw the man of the hour. Thor was there with his face a bright red as he cleared his throat.

"Hey, I, uh, didn't know you were here." He avoided eye contact and said, "Lyron was going to search for you."

"Give me a moment," I said, seeing the water was cooling down to a tolerable temperature. "My hands were wrinkling up, anyway."

I quickly dried off and changed, feeling unrushed as Thor simply looked the other way. The tips of his ears were red too. Poor guy. Walking by him, I patted his shoulder.

"Sorry, I didn't mean to kick you out," he said, still avoiding my eyes.

"You act like you've never seen a woman," I scoffed. Despite his looks, decency, and strength, he appeared more awkward than before. "Oh, I didn't mean that in a bad way. I just presumed you had been with a woman. Sorry."

"Nah, I just haven't found the right one, really. I was asked, but it never worked out," he exhaled. "Anyway, I stink from days out in the wild lands, and Lyron wants to talk to you."

"Okay," I said, as he dismissed the conversation altogether. "Welcome back though." He nodded, but still didn't look at me.

Walking up the hill, I was puzzled by the conversation at the hot springs. We had gotten along fine, with no awkwardness before he left. I was lost in thought, wondering what had changed, as I reached the top of the stairs. As if I didn't have enough of a headache, Lyron was standing there with his arms folded with a finger tapping on his other bicep.

"Did you have a nice bath?" he asked in an impatient tone, one I had never heard from him before. It was bitter, but not in a biting way.

"I did, until I was interrupted because you wanted to talk to me," I said, raising my eyebrows as I took the towel from around my shoulders and squeezed my hair.

"Time to train. Are you ready?"

"Seriously? I just bathed. Fine," I groaned. I didn't want to miss training, but I was owed another bath later.

Lyron turned around and for a moment we walked in silence as I brooded over my shortened bath followed by the summoning of training. I noticed Lyron move his head a few times as if he wanted to talk to me, but he didn't. I raised an eyebrow when our eyes met for a moment before he finally broke the silence.

The words came carefully, only a slight hitch in his tone. "Did he see you?" he asked.

The heat that colored my cheeks could be felt to my toes. The question left me stunned and my words stuttered out. That was the last question I expected. "I hardly think that's your business. Even if he did, what would it matter?"

As we reached the empty hall, I looked up and Lyron's piercing gaze struck every nerve in my body. The aura that flooded from him was primal. I stopped, and he followed suit as he turned around. His body stalked mine as I backed up. My body reacted on its own as the cool stone scratched my back. His hands braced on either side of my head as he leaned forward, his eyes level with mine.

His voice was controlled, taking his time making sure none of his words lost their meaning. "Plucking his eyes from his head would be a downfall to my scouting. I hardly wish for it to come to that. However, if you desired him to see you, then that would be another implication," Lyron said.

Taking in a couple of deep breaths, I reached up and grabbed his collar and pulled him forward so our lips were almost touching. He wouldn't have the upper hand, so I made sure to speak in a level and clear voice. "My body is mine to give away, or keep from whoever and whatever I wish. If I wished to spread my legs for Thor, I would not wait for your approval. Obviously, you lack the understanding of timing. For him to come down there on your orders and for you to be waiting, that would be a quick moment of passion. Not worth the wait for a lover who was gone for days. I will not give you an explanation for who I desire or what I desire unless it implicates our arrangement."

Letting go of his collar, I tilted my head while raising my eyebrow for understanding. His eyes widened, and he cleared his throat before standing straight. "Right, then. Training."

"Yes, training," I agreed, looking forward to today's lesson. I already learned one interesting thing, Lyron was jealous.

Fighting was not something I grew up with. It was learned much later when I fled the Desert Order. Remembering the first time I encountered Desmond's men was a lesson I almost didn't learn from. That day, I learned to cauterize a wound to keep me from bleeding out. While fire normally would not hurt a Firan, hot metal from a knife still did the trick. The technicalities of the different abilities still mystified me. The Desert Order believed it was the moon goddess' will, but my grandmother thought otherwise. I remember being very confused.

"Your gift comes from mutation and evolution. Human kind was forced to survive, and it did in the only way it knew how, to change and perhaps absorb properties. It's a theory, but it fits as most powers are regional. The moon goddess' illusion calms the hearts of those who didn't know where to turn. The moon is a powerful sight, fearful if you're like me, and remember when it was nearly the size of a fingernail in the sky. Now, even in daylight, it is constant. The pieces ever falling into the sea and land below."

Knocked to the ground, I cursed for being distracted. The flattened dirt floor covered my clothes and hair in brown specks as I stood up and shook it off, ready to go on the offensive. I dived to Lyron and swept my legs under his feet. Catching him off guard, I pounced as my wooden blade aimed above his throat.

I did it... I won a match.

Staring in disbelief, he laid there, shocked as I straddled his legs and held down his shoulder with my free hand. My brother showed me how to defend myself. He was a capable fighter, and he would have liked Lyron and Thor.

"That was new," Lyron said, catching his breath.

"My brother was in the Desert Order's trackers and taught me that before Desmond took over. Just kind of happened," I said, standing up and reaching my hand out. Lyron took it and smiled.

"Your brother sounds like he cared for his younger sister," he said as he patted his clothes, dirt clouding around him as he did so.

"He did," I said, remembering the little moments we had. The way Cyrus would share his food when he found extra fruit at the market, the way he patted my head when I was frustrated, the way he always told me he was proud of me. Even if I did nothing but help our mother with housework. "Desmond took him, too. Another reason to lure him out of hiding. You said Thor was bringing back a prisoner?"

"Yes, he's kept deep in the dungeon maze. Even if he did escape he will never find daylight unless we will it," Lyron said firmly. In other words, don't try to find him yourself or do anything foolish. "I will question him later to see if he is willing to share anything about our enemy. You will be there in the darkness to validate his claims."

"I may not know everything, but at least we have a plan." Lyron was turning around to put his wooden sword away. "Wait, are you done already? I finally won and you're done just like that?" Frustration and annoyance played in my mind. Sore loser.

Lyron laughed, a deep laugh from his gut that I hadn't heard before. "You have proven to me you can fight well, and even a bit dirty but at least your technique is fixed. We have much to do, so let's see if it was a mishap another time. Next, we work on speed."

"Goodie," I grumbled as he made long strides to leave the hall while I eagerly tried to keep up.

His kind words warmed my heart. He thought of me as capable. I hadn't heard those words since my brother.

"The questioning will not happen until after the festival. I have no reason to fear my position being compromised and there is much to prepare for. I will not be able to train with you until after that. However, there is someone who's been wanting to meet you and I trust fully in my absence. His name is Oak and his wife is Sunny," Lyron casually said making me come to a stop.

"Oak, the one who I nearly killed?" I asked bewildered. Lyron stopped to turn to me.

"Ah, yes, he looks forward to seeing how you've improved," he said with clear humor as his eyes sparked interest and his lips curved into a smirk. "He harbors no ill will. He complimented your headbutt wholeheartedly."

Continuing to walk out of the hall, my face twisted in a myriad of emotions. Confusion mostly as I wondered just how hard I hit Oak's head. Also, what kind of strange person compliments a headbutt?

"Sounds ominous," I grumbled as Lyron shook his head. Clearing my throat, I wondered about our earlier encounter. What would it matter to him if Thor was interested? What did it matter to me? I had no need for a hero, I didn't want to owe a man anything so high as my life. "Just to be clear,

Thor didn't see anything. He told me when I first came if I wanted a hero talk to him. If I wanted someone to make the hard decision come to you. His honor wouldn't let him even if he wanted to."

"He said that, did he?" Lyron mused, stopping for a moment. "He does seem to think he's a bit of a hero, and I guess he is all things considered." I caught up to him as he continued. "But don't doubt he is also a man."

"I am aware. I stopped counting on men as heroes. The last one that said he was my hero died and saved me from nothing," I said as I blew a breath out. Swinging my arms above my head I clasped them behind my neck and stretched.

"How do you view men?" Lyron muttered.

"Mostly a bother, but I think not all of them are bad. So long as they're honest," I said walking forward. We continued walking out of the hall.

"I'll see you at the events, Milana," he called out behind me. His footsteps halted, but I kept my pace. Unclasping my hands I waved my fingers without looking back.

Taking a deep breath, I found myself alone for the first time in ages. People walked near me and said a quick greeting as I moved my way through the quiet halls. The sun was far enough in the sky to almost be dinner time, but I had time to spare. No Ivy, no Thor, no Lyron for the first time since I arrived. As much as I came to enjoy some company, this was a refreshing change.

"Look at that smile. Did you gut a man to death today?" I heard Tucker laugh as he waved me over to his stand.

"Do I look that menacing?" I asked, feigning hurt feelings, touching a hand to my chest and frowning.

"No, you just look that happy. Figured you castrated that little idiot," he whispered with a devilish grin. Without much said, I knew exactly who he was talking about.

Nearly choking on air, I stifled a laugh. "Ha, no. He just got back plus there is nothing I want to do with his lower region," I whispered back, raising my eyebrows as Tucker nodded.

"Probably for the best," Tucker nodded as he grabbed a kabob of food and handed it to me. "For your trouble. Happiness looks good on you, kid."

"Didn't realize I looked so chipper," I said, taking the stick with meat and rolled dumplings graciously as I closed my eyes to savor the flavors as the tender meat gave way.

"Better than when you first came here anyway. I've had a few folks ask about ya. Nothing too crazy just where you came from and if you planned to stay. I just tell em that you were a Wild and you'll stay as long as you see fit," he said, noting the worried look on my face.

"Let's keep it that way, shall we? I have a deal with Lyron and that's all. A common goal and when that's fulfilled, I plan on leaving." I leaned my backside against the side of the stall. A part of me felt empty when I talked about leaving, the other piece felt missing. As if I was trying to convince myself that I would leave. Staying here was not what I had wanted, but then it wasn't so bad... was it?

"Anything to do with the refugees Thor came in with? He brought them to the medical unit for the ladies to tend to. Only a few serious cases. That Desert Order trying to kidnap people and bring them in. That monster leader of theirs has been on a killing spree. Hardly anyone left to serve him from the rumors," Tucker said with a sigh and shaking his head.

My blood ran cold as my skin pricked up. Refugees were coming in and Lyron didn't tell me?

Desmond had never stopped killing, not that I expected him to. If I was more resourceful than, maybe I could have ended it? Maybe if Lyron weren't merciful, none of it would have happened in the first place. However, it didn't do any good to blame him or myself. We made a choice. It just so happened to have stained our hands with blood. Both of us had to live with that decision.

My appetite was gone, but I finished Tucker's offering. I put on a smile, but my heart was no longer in it. Every time I become happy and content, Desmond comes to destroy what small hope I have. I wandered to the lake where some members of the Order swam and played. I remained alone in my thoughts. Tucking my knees to my chest, I sat there trying to make sense of it all. A couple waved, but didn't approach from the water. A large man and a small woman with long wavy golden hair. The man had short brown hair. I waved my finger tips back at them, but I quickly tucked my chin into my knees letting my head rest on them.

No one bothered me, and I was grateful. But then I had to wonder... did anyone see me suffering?

My head snapped up and I shook my head. I was being foolish and selfish. Everyone had their own battle to bear. They had no business taking on mine as well. Walking quickly to the fortress, the sun had set already and I had missed dinner. Tucker's offering was more than enough and, I wasn't hungry. With the festival underway, I imagined everyone would be too busy to pay me much mind.

The next day, my stomach was tight and my mind was racing. Today I would officially meet the large ogre of a man I head-butted so hard I knocked him out for days on end. I hesitated to go to the arena, but realized it was silly. We were all adults here, and if someone couldn't get over a fight or flight reaction then they could kiss my ass.

"I knew it was her," I heard a woman exclaim in a high pitch. She was pointing at me and practically jumping up and down when I turned to look. The couple from the lake were Sunny and Oak.

"Seriously, of course you did. Ivy wouldn't shut up about her," Oak gruffed out as he rubbed his temple and shook his head.

"I'm so happy we get to meet, finally." Sunny bounded to me, clasping my hands with her small petite hands with long narrow fingers. Honestly, I had never met such a beautiful, dainty woman in all my life. And she was with... him.

Oak was burly and hulking, where she was elegant and petite. Until now, the notion of opposites attracting seemed far-fetched to me.

I hesitated, stumbling over the correct words. Never had I met a person who I nearly killed and not have them wanting to kill me back. Oak looked more annoyed with how close Sunny was rather than my presence. "Thank you. I'm sorry about, well, before."

"Nah, don't worry about it," Oak said as he ran his hand through his short, golden hair. "I'm just impressed your skull didn't crack. I have a little birdie tell me I have a hard head."

Sunny gave a 'hmph' and glared at him while sticking her tongue out. I couldn't help but smile at their exchange.

"Now, I hear we have some training to do. Little lady, I will make sure you can deliver better than headbutts," he said with a grin as he cracked his knuckles. Sunny stepped aside, releasing my hands with a smile. His confidence radiated as his demeanor changed. Clapping her hands a few times together, she bounded off to the side and sat, crossing her ankles in front of her.

"Kick his ass, Lana!" Lana?

With me distracted, he swung, and I barely dodged, falling to the ground.

"What the hell?" I yelled as I scrambled up as he kept swinging and steadily moving forward with every controlled punch.

"Distractions get you killed. I'm here to teach you close combat and how to maintain focus," he said with the out-breath of every punch. "Your enemy won't allow you time to get up. Either over power them or outsmart them."

And so began the days of torture with Oak and Sunny.

CHAPTER EIGHT — COMMITTED

<u>Lyron</u>

For three days, Milana had eluded me. Thor hadn't noticed her much, either. Ivy spotted her only during meals. She appeared fine when I left the hall with her, radiating high spirits. The festival kept me from asking if she was doing well. Oak and Sunny, too, remained scarce. Curiosity tempted me to visit her room only to not have an answer. However, by the next day, she was seen eating.

This woman threatened to unravel my sanity. The thought of her being in danger made my heart clench with fear. If I told her that, I'm sure she'd push me away. Somehow, she was more obstinate than me.

The morning of the festival arrived, and I was ready to receive some challenges. These events were more for public release of tension. Few from outside Orders came to partake, but sometimes a few Northern Order men would galivant in here. This year was no different as I saw them coming down the hall. Thor made sure everyone who entered was vouched for and known to us. If not, we took extra precautions for the safety of our people.

The first one was a man I knew well.

"Tank," I said, reaching out my hand. He took it and squeezed firmly. "Welcome back to our Order. I presume we get to spar again? Longer this time."

"Ha! You know you just caught me off guard last year. That ale your Order makes is good, made me slow." Tank was a good man who wanted adventure. The formality of the Orders bothered him, but the Northerners were more relaxed in terms of traditional rules. Their hierarchy changed frequently, but if a leader angered enough of them, they killed him off. Their leader was the mass majority vote, and I envied that sometimes.

Tank was a large, barrel-chested man with a squinty eyed grin. If anyone was mad at him, it wouldn't take them long to come around. He loved himself a good time and a good woman to warm his bed, that was what most knew about him. But beyond that he was a loyal man who would kill to protect those close to him.

"Then perhaps save the drinks for after the fight," I offered with a smirk as he put a hand on my shoulder and laughed.

"What fun would that be? Get drunk with me and we can have a really fun fight."

While greeting the other guests, I found Tank's offer more appealing. Year after year, these festivals drained my energy. Not to mention the festival after this where many would gather around the fire, dance, and then go find a room to be more private in. Finding myself in my room and avoiding the crowd became my tradition. The appeal of public fights didn't bother me. It was the political nature of these meetings with rumors of Order changing leadership that made me want to go drink a barrel of ale. However, I settled for one tankard just to loosen up enough to be friendly through the event.

Tank's voice perked up. "You're new here? I didn't see you last year, and I'd remember a face like yours."

Looking at him, my stomach sank. I excused myself from my current company and watched Milana back away from him, shaking her head. As he reached for her, my hand grasped his wrist.

My voice commanded his obedience and Tank's eyes widened. "I would leave her alone. Respectfully, this woman is a guest and will receive the respect she deserves."

"Crap, is she your woman?" he inquired, looking between the both of us. I straightened up and let his wrist go. As he rubbed his wrist, Milana's face reddened.

"As I said, she is a guest," I repeated, my jaw ticking.

"I am my own woman. I hardly need to be owned to have some respect, last I checked. Who the hell are you?"

I swear she was ready to knock him flat. Her stance was perfect, her body poised and ready—fluid. Oak did an excellent job fine tuning her training.

"Tank from the Northern Order. I foolishly challenge this guy every year for some good clean fighting fun," he said with a slight bow. By the way his tone turned formal, I would say he was transfixed. And I am not impressed.

"That's enough now," I said as he takes his time getting up from his bow. "You can go find someone else to bother until I secure my fist in your face."

Shaking his head, he smiled with a twinkle in his eye. "Promises, promises, Lyr." Turning around, he nodded to Milana before heading off.

"How was training?" I ask Milana now that Tank was out of earshot.

"You didn't tell me he was obsessed with fighting," she gritted, smiling with a death glare.

Trying to resist the urge to laugh, I smirk and leaned down to her ear. "You didn't ask."

Her cheeks flush into a brilliant red, clearing her throat. I enjoy the effect I have on her.

"I suppose I didn't. But he seemed awfully eager to make sure I hurt at least once a day, if not the whole day. I'm surprised I can even walk," Milana muttered as she crossed her arms.

"Lana!"

Sunny wrapped herself around Milana's arm and hugged for a moment before releasing her. Oak would eventually catch up. He always did.

"You've made a new friend," I remarked, gesturing to their closeness.

Sunny waved dismissively, her smile bright. "Lana didn't have a choice with me. I like her and that's that. Not many can lay that ogre flat on his ass for days, and I admire a strong woman. I hope Kira eats dirt." I almost spat out my drink.

Milana looked stronger, more sure of herself. Whatever Oak did, I certainly noticed a difference. Ferocity and confidence radiated from her, even with the ordeal with Tank. Thor thought she needed saving. I disagreed. She needed to be honed like a blade for war. A woman like her was not to be underestimated. Instead of being weary about her, I felt a surge of pride.

Oak finally joined us, his gaze fixed on me. "They're ready to get started. Shall we go?"

"If we must," I said as the ladies walked behind Oak and in front of me.

Sunny gently rubbed Milana's arm. "You'll do fine. Don't be nervous and just kick ass out there, Lana."

Nodding her head, Milana's shoulders expanded with her breath and contracted.

"Yeah, this little spitfire learns fast. No wonder you wanted me to spar with her," Oak said, tilting his head so I can see his smirk.

Pride surged within me once more, and I wholeheartedly agreed. She learned fast. In this world, you had to or you died. The will to live with her was stronger than most. Even my own did not match. Perhaps when I left the Mountain Order, it would have rivaled. Leadership took the wind from the sails, so to speak.

"I'll take her where she needs to go. Have fun, Lyr," Sunny said as she waved me off.

Fun... Maybe it *would* be fun in the arena.

Everyone gathered in the circles surrounding the arena. The levels from the ground to the fifth were filled with people rushing to find a place. Many familiar faces filled the room, while some were new to me. Among them, I noticed Thor taking his place beside me, and on the other side sat Kira. Our seats were on the second level, and there were three stone chairs for us to sit. Usually there was little sitting.

"Welcome, everyone," I said, my voice carrying across the arena. The hush settled over the crowd like a heavy blanket, as I drew in a deep breath.

"I thank you for being here for the festivities. In most Orders this is seen as a time of turmoil and an uprising can happen. However, under this tradition, we have watched children grow up smiling and laughing. People living without fear, and a time of peace where in most of the Orders there are none."

As I spoke, smiles and nods of agreement rippled through the audience, and a sense of unity began to form.

"That being said, a challenger can approach at any time for combat and the crowd cheers their approval or their discontent with the match. Based on that reaction, it shall proceed or fall to the wayside."

Cheers filled the air, as I raised my hand. Within a moment, the crowd grew quiet again.

"You are also welcome to challenge anyone for a spot on Thor's team this year. Enjoy yourselves. Remember this is not a fight to the death. If a death looks imminent, you will be stopped."

I gestured to five men at the arena's side, ordering them to prevent any incidents. This was meant to be a celebration of strength, not a bloodbath of mourning. "Let us begin!"

The roar of the crowd erupted as the first fight began, a couple of men vying for a place on Thor's scouting team. Kira leaned over to me and I tilted my head in her direction.

"I hear your little desert princess wants to challenge me," she said, her pitch low and grasping for information, using a seductive tone. "I welcome her to try."

"Whatever your issue with her, it ends with that challenge if that is what happens. Or it simply ends today. I will not have my third act like a child, or I will just replace you to end this headache. Understood?"

Immediately, she shrank back in her seat, and my body was itching to fight Tank. Taking in a deep breath, I finished off my tankard and set it to the ground beside my chair. Thor had stood up to watch the fight, cheering with a smile on his face.

The skirmish with the Desert Order had reduced his scout numbers; as we grew more resourceful and cunning, they did too. A fact that bothered him and myself. The worry of an insider leaking information was unlikely, but not impossible.

Cheers erupted again as winners were chosen and more fights took off. Milana was below the arena with Sunny where fighters prepared. Still, my gaze wandered to hers. It didn't surprise me that Kira knew Milana was from the desert, her complexion and dark hair were giveaways. Conversations buzzed around me, as expected. The refugees may have recognized her, but the thought was pushed to the back of my mind.

Milana emerged from the underground pit and surprise overtook me. She wore a snug-fitting shirt, its sleeves exposing her bandaged arms. They were tucked into tight fitting lower wear that came to just above her knees. Her feet bandaged, but free to move and feel the ground beneath her. Much like Oak's general wear, I smirked at the realization that even though she was poised to fight, she still impressed me. Not even needing to fight, I saw her strength and willpower. I was not the only one immersed in her aura. Thor was aware of it too.

My chest burned as he waved to her, her less enthusiastic response offering a small comfort. I didn't want him looking at her...admiring her.

I didn't think about the revelation of those thoughts as Milana's voice called out a familiar name.

"Kira!"

Kira looked at me and shrugged. Standing and leaning over the side of the rail, she tried to look as bored as possible.

"Yes, princess?" Kira mocked loudly, and I cleared my throat as a warning.

"I wish to challenge you. You think of me as a waste of time for our leader and others. I wish to prove you wrong," Milana said, and the crowd cheered.

"You want my place, newbie? You're in over your head," Kira snapped.

"I don't give two shits about your spot. What I care about is shutting you up. If you respect me at the end—*great*, but I won't have you *disrespect* me."

"So be it," Kira said, walking towards the stairs.

The crowd cheered. Taking her time, she baited the anticipation. I could see Sunny whisper words to Milana, and she nodded in return. For a moment, Milana looked nervous, but quickly, her eyes gleamed with determination and her body bounced from foot to foot.

Mostly, everyone possessed well-toned bodies, but the way her body swayed made me see her as not only a woman, but a warrior. A woman worth fighting for. Standing, I leaned towards the rail and took in a deep breath. She was strong and fragile, quick-witted, and yet naïve, perfectly imperfect.

"Something wrong, Lyron?" Thor asked and I tilted my head towards him, never taking my eyes off her.

"Nothing, just realized something interesting," I murmured.

Thor winced and drew closer. "What was that? It's kind of loud," Thor asked.

"It's nothing. Just interested in how it'll go." I clapped my hands, and the hall fell silent after Kira made her way to the arena.

"While this is not a request for a position, the people have willed this fight to happen," I announced. "I'll remind the participants that this is not a fight to the death, but simply a show of strength. May the favor of the goddess smile upon you both." I raised my hands, then dropped them to my sides as Milana threw the first blow.

She unleashed a relentless barrage of attacks as Kira expertly dodged. Her body remained just ahead of Milana's with every strike and step forward. Only when she was nearly backed against the wall did she duck and strike Milana's lower ribs. As Milana knelt on the ground, Kira took side steps to create some distance.

"Is that all you've got? Pathetic," Kira taunted and spat on the ground.

Milana said nothing, then rose and shook her arms and head. She raised her arms, moving lightly on her feet, never firmly planting them as she closed in on Kira. Kira gestured with two fingers for her to come forward.

Milana punched forward but delivered an unexpected undercut that struck Kira in the jaw by her ear. The taunting stopped then. The dance between them continued, strike, dodge, strike, blow landed and so on. Learning each other's habits and moves, I was entranced by Milana's ability to adapt. Some of her fighting skills she learned from me, some from Oak, and others were all her own. Or perhaps from her brother.

I wondered about him. The admiration Milana had for him was envious, and I pondered if I would ever sit down for a drink with him and talk about the world. That fantasy ended as Milana was struck in the jaw. Blood seeped from her mouth and she spit out what she could, but Kira kept advancing. Blow after blow, Milana defended herself by curling up as Kira knelt on the ground for the onslaught.

About to call the fight, Milana extended her leg out and delivered a powerful kick to Kira's ribs. Putting Kira off balance, Milana struggled to move out of the way. However, it wasn't enough. Kira seized Milana's shoulders, brought her down, and straddled her upper body, pinning Milana's legs down.

"Enough!" I yelled over the crowd as Kira prepared for the final blow. I had seen more than enough.

Kira, her face and body battered like Milana's, slowly moved away from her. Milana spat blood and then clutched her ribs, using her other arm to push herself up.

"I trust this is enough of a show that Milana is not a hindrance to our Order, but an asset," I called out as a few cheered in the crowd.

"This was not an offer of position, but Kira holds her third in command, regardless. However, I have decided that Milana will become my bodyguard. There is a danger that lurks and I find it wise to have a strong, loyal warrior beside me and our leadership. If she agrees, that is."

Kira's mouth nearly dropped to the floor. Milana's eyes widened as she looked at Sunny, who was beaming ear to ear and shaking Oak's arm with excitement.

Thor whispered behind me through gritted teeth, "Lyron, is this really appropriate now?"

I held my hand up to him. This was not a discussion for now. In fact, his opinion mattered little to me right then. I was perfectly capable of fighting for myself. I just wanted any excuse to keep her close.

This woman would be the death of me.

Chapter Nine - Fighting Herself

<u>Milana</u>

I stood there, bruised and battered, as the reality sank in.

Lyron's bodyguard.

Sunny eyes sparkled with excitement, a stark contrast to my dumbstruck gaze. Judging by the audible gasp from the crowd, this was unheard of. The hesitant applause that followed rang hollow in my ears. *Was this a dream or a nightmare?* I wanted to owe this man nothing, to keep our precarious distance in check. However, with a single order, he demolished it.

But then, it wasn't an order.

His request took me off guard because an order from a leader was absolute. His amendment of my agreement blinded and muted me to everyone but him. Azure blue eyes locked onto me, pleading for me to say yes. My jaw quivered as I waged war between wanting to keep my freedom and wanting to belong here.

I longed for the wilderness. To be in the silence of nature. But, I found a place to rest my head and had adjusted to human companionship, little by little. Comfortable in the silence, I'd remained a step ahead of Desmond's men most of the time. Here, I put my trust in those who could betray me. Yet, under Lyron's gaze and Thor's stern observation, a connection began to form within me. A yearning to stay a little longer.

After the crowd quieted to mere murmurs, I nodded my head and said, "I agree."

The smile radiating from Lyron made my heart beat faster. I stared at him as Sunny ran to me and grabbed my arm, pulling me to the side of the arena. Fluttering with excitement, she gushed over each move I made against Kira. The woman was a fierce opponent. Oak taught me some of her fighting style, but as I learned her ways, she learned mine. Her last punch would have knocked me out if Lyron hadn't stepped in.

Part of me resented he did. The other sliver of me was grateful that I only had to heal up my ribs, jaw, and a slightly swollen eyebrow. When I fought, I felt the flames dance within me with pride, the warrior within me flickering to life. As the afterglow of the fight permeated the air, Sunny led me down below the arena, where wooden benches surrounded a well, offering a welcome respite.

"That was amazing!" Sunny whispered-yelled as she washed my eye with a damp rag. Oak kept guard over the area since there was a buzz among the crowd for my new position. Most people remained above for the fights, but I was grateful for the peace and quiet.

"I got my ass beat," I grumbled, feeling a sting where she passed over with the rag, and hissing at the touch.

"Sorry about that." Sunny grimaced, moving my jaw gently between her index and thumb to get a better look at the damage. "But to be fair, she didn't look good either."

"Lyron must be on edge," Oak said from the doorway. "He's never done that."

"What do you think that means?" Sunny asked curiously. "I've never seen him take an interest in adding extra guards, let alone a bodyguard."

"It means he wants to keep her close, that's all I know. The rest is just a hunch," Oak said with a shrug. He glanced at me with a smirk. "You did good. I was impressed you kept up that long. Kira fights dirty, and she adapts easily. Looks like we have another female fighter on our hands who can do the same. Knocking you down as much as I did made you able to get up fast."

I hissed again as Sunny pressed against my ribs. "Yeah, thanks I guess."

"You're going to be resting for a while. If they're not broken, they'll hurt even worse. Bruised ribs are hell," Sunny lamented, shaking her head.

"I've had worse," I said, shrugging. I had dealt with situations like these countless times, narrowly escaping capture, enduring beatings, and facing near-death experiences. "I'd like to watch the others fight, though." This is the first time I watched fights for sport rather than gain. "I'm curious."

Sunny opened her mouth to protest before Oak smiled ear to ear. "Can't hurt none. May as well have her take notes since she's a quick study," Oak reasoned before Sunny could argue, motioning for me to follow.

Slowly moving behind Oak and in front of Sunny, they helped me dodge the inquisitive souls. Looking up to where Kira sat, I felt a little better. She looked like hell. None too happy, either. Smirking, it was hard to keep from smiling. My gaze was drawn to Lyron, who raised an eyebrow and shook his head, a subtle, amused smile tugging at the corner of his mouth. He turned his attention to Thor, who was talking coarsely with him. His brows pinched together and his jaw was tense, the displeasure in their conversation obvious. Regardless, Thor waved him off and uttered a few words before they both straightened. I caught Thor's glance, but he looked away just as fast.

Ah! He was not happy with the fight. I understood it, but he didn't feel what Kira said and my body ached to release tension. I didn't need his protection, despite his belief. The yearning to fight my own battles won. And now that I had that taste, I didn't want to go back to the helpless girl Desmond pushed around. For the first time in my life, I felt stronger than anyone. Ironic considering how beaten and battered I was.

My eyes returned to Lyron, and I noticed that Tank, who'd approached me earlier, had now clasped his hand on Lyron's shoulder, wearing a bright smile. I grimaced, not liking his ease around Lyron. I could understand the confusion regarding Lyron's reaction earlier; it surprised me how swiftly he had intervened, especially considering his distance from me in the room. To most, such interference would imply a claim of partnership, as women usually handled unwanted advances themselves.

I remembered once, at the Earth Order, the very brief time I was there, how a woman cried out, running out of her hut with her clothes in tatters. Dragging the man out of the house, other men in the Order beat him to death right there in the middle of the day. His screaming and pathetic attempts to fight off five men fell on deaf ears. As far as they were concerned, he deserved his fate. Can't say I thought different. Life is a series of choices and he made his and met his fate accordingly.

Fate. Such a strange word to suddenly believe in.

Tank walked down the path Kira had taken earlier and saw me. Holding out his arms, he approached but couldn't get past Oak. I smirked and shook my head.

"What a fight, little lady. Now it's time for your partner to get into the arena with me. If I win, will you come to the Northern Order?" He winked at me. Oak shook his head and pinched the bridge of his nose.

"I think I'd rather stay here. I just got promoted after all," I said, seeing Lyron approach with his eyes burning into Tank.

Tank turned around and patted Lyron on the back. "I like your little lady. She's a spitfire."

"You have no idea," Lyron murmured, shaking his head. "Let's get this over with. I have much to discuss with my new bodyguard, Thor and Kira."

A booming laugh filled the air as Tank walked away from us. Sunny and Oak rolled their eyes and groaned. Looking between them, I raised an eyebrow.

"He's always so crude," Sunny said, taking my arm, and leading me through the crowd toward Thor. Not exactly where I wanted to be, but with Sunny and Oak I had little to worry about. Ivy was scarce today, which felt strange considering she was normally my shadow.

Oak kept us a short distance from Thor. Kira seemed to be out of sight. Maybe getting her split lip taken care of. At least I could say I landed a few punches on her. Considering Oak's reaction, I called it a victory. It gave the impression I was not to be underestimated. Sunny released my arm and leaned forward on the rail to watch Tank and Lyron go down.

Oak pointed down to the arena and said, "He does this every year. Says he wants to be stronger, so he keeps challenging

Lyron. Never won a fight yet, but then I think he enjoys the pain. This will be over fast."

"So why does he keep coming back?"

"For fun. So he says."

I knew many guys who fought for fun. Teenage boys with nothing better to do. Not a Leader and someone who enjoyed losing every year, never in an arena like this. However, by the sound of the crowd cheering, it was more for fun than anything. Tank was revving up the crowd as Lyron stretched quietly off to the side.

"I'm baaaack," Tank sang out as the crowd erupted. Once they quieted down, he continued. "As every year comes, I am here to challenge your Leader. Lyron has been a good teacher of strength and patience. Too bad I've only listened to one lesson."

Laughter radiated through the crowd as Tank went into a fighting stance. Lyron simply stood there, waiting. Tank was twice as muscular, but about the same height as Lyron.

Lyron's long, black hair was neatly braided to keep it out of the way, yet he appeared utterly unfazed by Tank's presence, his expression betraying nothing but boredom. Fascinated, I leaned forward to see Tank shifting his weight from leg to leg. In a taunting gesture, Lyron brought up his hand and flexed his fingers, beckoning Tank to come forward.

What happened next defied any logical explanation.

As Tank closed the gap between them, Lyron's movements seemed effortless, as if he had encountered no resistance at all. With a swift motion, Lyron grabbed Tank's arm, lifting him into the air and flipping him over, causing Tank to land on his back with a gasp for air. After giving Tank some space, Lyron shook his head and knelt down, uttering something incomprehensible. It appeared as though he said, 'I warned you.' Tank managed a weak laugh and slowly rose to his feet, bracing himself on his knees.

Oak stifled a laugh and shook his head. "Tank shouldn't have bothered you. Now it's personal, like tempting a bull."

"What do you mean?" I asked, not taking my eyes from Lyron as he easily avoided Tank's advances.

"Sunny, this one is on you," Oak said, as he watched the fight with a smirk.

"Lyron has a soft spot for you, and few have the pleasure of saying that. He protects all of us, but Tank went and pushed his hospitality," Sunny explained with a smile.

"There shouldn't be a reason to though, we have an understanding," I said, shaking my head. Lyron never said he had feelings, we just had encounters that were slightly awkward.

"My dear, dear Lana, I mean to say that Lyron likes you as more than just one of his people. You're special to him.

What kind of special remains to be determined, but with everyone seeing how Tank talked to you, he's setting an example," Sunny said with a sigh as she gestured to the fight.

Thor was closer to us now as he leaned over the rail. "Stop filling her head with bullshit. Lyron is simply looking out for her," he quipped as Oak squared up as a barrier between me and him.

"I'm not the one in denial, Thor. Lyron is toying with Tank more so than previous years," Oak said, folding his arms.

Thor shook his head and remained silent as we turned our attention back to the fight.

Lyron's gaze briefly shifted to me before he used Tank as a makeshift tool to catapult himself, narrowly avoiding a direct attack. His eyes then darted toward Thor for a moment, but soon returned to me. Turning his back on us, he engaged in a few more passes with Tank before shaking his head, growing tired of the fight, while Tank was visibly out of breath.

There was an exchange of words between the fighters before Lyron charged at Tank. Employing his legs to launch himself upward, he collided his calf into Tank's shoulder, sending him crashing to the ground. The crowd gasped before erupting into cheers for their Leader. It puzzled me why he needed a bodyguard at all. Suddenly, the aura of invincibility that had surrounded me began to crumble.

Sunny put her arms around my shoulders and whispered in my ear, "Are you okay?"

I looked away from Lyron and turned to her with a half smile. "Yeah, I'm fine. Just a little worn out suddenly."

"Let's take you somewhere more quiet, this will go on for a couple of days." Sunny then led me to my room with Oak trailing behind. The halls were nearly empty, but the outside marketplace was more lively than ever. Passing by the open arches on our way back to the living quarters, I could see the bustle of the crowd.

A couple of days? I could only imagine the team needed to secure this place. Everything was going smoothly, so I didn't make it my problem to worry about it. At least, I didn't want to. However, all these people put me on edge, as if Desmond could invade at any moment. It would be my luck that the one place I stayed at for longer than a few days would be the place that ensured my demise.

Sunny fussed with my pillows so I could be comfortable, and promised she or Ivy would be in to check on me. Oak reminded me I did well and to rest up. There would be plenty of time to train later. Sleep took over quickly, but not without the nightmares.

"You'll never escape me." I could hear Desmond's taunt as an icy chill woke me. My body covered in sweat through my clothes, I took in gasping breaths. A hand covered my mouth, and I screamed as tears threatened to form.

But these hands were dainty, feminine.

"Shhh..., it's okay," the woman whispered as my eyes adjusted. "I can't believe it's you."

Her hand moved away from my mouth as my heart rate came back to a steady pulse. I tried to squint my eyes to get a better look, but her face was too shrouded in shadow.

"Who are you?" I whispered.

"Oh, goodness. I'm sorry. I wanted to make sure you were okay, but that was less than an ideal first impression. You probably don't remember me, but I was your brother's best friend's little sister, Remi."

My memory took a moment, but I remembered her as a little girl. She was so young then when I ran away. Her voice had the same melodic quality and her body looked similar to Sunny's. She was small, and I'd become protective of her when our brothers would pick on her.

"Remi?" I lurched forward, my ribs revolting in pain, and hugged her. Tears sprang from my eyes, and hers too. The sobs filled my room, but they were so joyous. We made it. We survived the monster that took our beautiful home away from us. "I heard there were refugees here. Are you one of them?"

She nodded, wiping her tears as she moved to feel my face with her hands. I cupped her cheeks with my hands and noticed a scar by her eyes. I flicked my wrist to light a candle, and I gasped.

The scar went across her face, her eyes permanently shut. The skin warped and twisted from another Firan. Anger heated through my body. "Who did it? I'll kill them."

"It's done. My brother made sure of it," she said as she patted my hand that held her face.

"Is he here?"

"He is," she said, and I sighed in relief. "He wanted to watch the fights, which is where we saw you. I can't believe you're Lyron's bodyguard. That's so amazing. I always knew you were strong, stronger than anyone, Firan or no."

"I'm not," I huffed. "His fight made me feel so weak when I watched him with that guy, Tank." My ego from earlier was deflated as I remembered how effortlessly Lyron moved and overtook a man so much larger than him.

Her hand that remained on my face shook with a gentle nudge. "You fought against someone who you had never fought against before, against the odds, and took a stand. Don't sell yourself short," she said as she came in to rest her head on my shoulder. "Does it hurt?"

I let out a quick puff of air to laugh. "Yes, but it's worth it."

"Still the same. Stubborn and never one to back down," she said with a quiet giggle.

"I suppose so." I smiled back as I rested my head on hers for a moment before we started talking.

Memories were shared about our time at the Desert Order, and her life with her brother, Maki, and their journey here. The memories of fruit in the market, the nights between our houses as I watched Remi countless times as our parents would dance the night away at the festivals, and our brothers constantly stirring up trouble with a smile on their faces. Memories I had forgotten, innocent moments of a cut-short childhood.

Maki and Cyrus were always together, and my brother's death nearly killed him, too. The anger that boiled in our blood never wavered. I just had to hide mine better because of my Firan abilities. Anger always ignited an uncontrollable burst of energy, as if it had to go somewhere and take out anyone near, as if to try to give me peace.

The night flew by, and daybreak was on the horizon. My yawns were catching up with me as Remi's talks about the past became less enthusiastic. We were both exhausted. Falling asleep next to me was a close fit, but we found a comfortable spot back to back. I had a friend once more. A devoted friend who knew me in my darkest hour and still was so happy to see me. Five years of not knowing anyone was truly lonely. For a long time, I never admitted it. Remi made me remember just why I fought to hold on. To save those like her who were too young to go through what I did.

I woke up to Remi humming a lullaby. One that our mothers would always sing to us, the melody haunting yet beautiful. I could never do it justice. Remi was talented in that way, her singing voice as melodic as her speaking voice. At least the monsters that took her eyes didn't take that from her.

"Good morning," she said, lifting her head up and turning towards me. She was sitting by the window, her hand outside, feeling the warmth of the sun.

"Wish it was a little less of a painful morning," I said, slumping back down, stretching gently, and feeling every rib cry out in protest.

"Well, that's the price you pay for strength, right?" she said with a giggle. A saying that Cyrus said a lot back when Maki and he would spar.

"Yeah, yeah."

"I'll go get us breakfast. Want me to bring Maki up?" As she moved with ease around my room, I wondered about the burn to her eyes.

Once she reached the door, she picked up a thin walking stick that was leaning against the wall. I saw so much of her mother in her, such poise and grace. I was always envious that I seemed so boyish. Being corrected constantly for not being prim and proper, and even more so after Desmond took over to hide me in the crowd. But Remi, Maki, and Cyrus never held it against me I was different.

"That sounds good. I'd like to see him," I said as she beamed a huge smile.

"Perfect, see you soon," she said, using the stick to maneuver outside of the room.

Closing my eyes, I rested and let my Firan abilities work their magic. Healing was an advantage I had. Somehow I could concentrate on a spot and heal it faster. A warming sensation would tingle and that's when it took hours to heal instead of days. My ribs flexed and ached as the heat moved through my body, investigating anything out of the ordinary. It took great concentration, but it was worth it when I heard a knock on my door.

"Come in," I called out, thinking it was Remi. Strange, considering she broke into my room last night.

"You seem cheerful," Lyron said with a smirk.

My eyes widened as I realized my error. "Well, I was expecting a friend to bring my breakfast. One of your refugees, actually, Remi and Maki."

"Maki is a man," he said, narrowing his eyes.

I smirked and raised an eyebrow. "Jealous? Of a man who has been a long-time friend and the closest person I have to a brother?"

"Ah, I see," he said, and sat down at my table. "Well, I was just checking in on you. Kira is still on the mend, but I see you are faring far better. One of your abilities?"

"Yes, Firans are good healers. I was already working on that," I said, sitting up and crossing my leg. Learning forward, I tilted my head as I gauged him. He appeared at ease with his hair braided, yet regal. Like he was meant for leadership. "Why the bodyguard ruse?"

"Who said it was a ruse?" he countered.

"It seems unnecessary."

"If we intend to spend a lot of time together and avoid any public misconceptions about us being a couple, I believed this was the only way to draw that clear line," he explained, taking a deep breath.

"Hm, I suppose you have a point. I'd hate to constantly beat every woman who wants to have a chance at your heart or your bed," I said with a grin. "Not that I want it, but I'd hate for there to be confusion."

"Not that you want it, indeed." Lyron sighed, shaking his head. "Honestly, you'd be doing me a favor by taking the title, regardless. Everyone now knows how strong of a competitor you are. That's not a light compliment. You're a fighter, and any man would be lucky to have you."

"Well, thank you. I'll keep it in mind when I want to deal with the complexities of relationships. In the meantime, you can go back to your fights and I will continue waiting for my breakfast. You are dismissed, fearless leader," I said as I flicked my fingers for him to go.

He smiled and let out a breathy laugh. "You are truly something else, Milana. I look forward to our arrangement." Walking out of the door, he held it open for Remi and nodded to Maki. Maki held the door for his sister and smiled at me. He held my tray of food and set it on the table before coming to me.

"I couldn't believe it was you," he said after the door shut. He was gentle as he wrapped me in his arms. "Remi said you were hurt, but I see you did the trick to take care of that. That'a girl."

I smiled as I looked at the food Maki had brought. Fresh fruits, oatmeal, and what looked like a cup of steaming tea called to me. "Thank you for bringing this up. I appreciate it. Sorry for Lyron, he was just stopping by to check in."

"Nah, the guy is scary, but he doesn't give off psycho vibes," Maki said, looking to the door. "Actually seems like a good guy. Cyrus would approve."

"There's nothing to approve. We have an arrangement and that's all. Nothing romantic."

"Yeah, okay. That look he gave me said otherwise. It said 'lay off my woman, you swine'. Definitely some touch-her-and-die going on," Maki said, shivering as Remi laughed.

Remi pushed her brother's shoulder. "If anything, Cyrus would have liked him for that alone," Remi said. Maki laughed and nodded.

I missed my brother deeply, and somehow, these two individuals made me feel like he was still here—a living, breathing memory that came naturally and vividly to me. My brother had been protective, especially after I discovered I was a Firan, the only woman with this unique ability. Why that was, I had no idea, as no other woman had ever admitted to having it. Those who controlled Air, known as Airians, and Earth, known as Terrans, had no such gender-skewed abilities. However, those who wielded Water, called Aquans, were mostly women. This thought lingered in the back of my mind. Perhaps I was simply more masculine than most women, given my enjoyment of throwing punches; it wouldn't be a far-fetched notion.

I smirked, looking at Remi and Maki, who were sharing smiles and glances with each other. "What is it?" I asked.

"Just seems like you're happy here," Remi said, reaching out her hand to mine. I took her graceful, delicate fingers in my callused ones.

"I'd be happy too if I had a Leader in my corner," Maki muttered as Remi swatted him with her free hand.

"Oh, shut it. He cares for her, and that's what matters most," Remi chastised.

"Actually, there's nothing romantic about it. We both want to kill Desmond, so this thing about me being his bodyguard is really about me being the bait to lure him out of the Desert Order. This is just part of the plan, although he didn't tell me at first," I admitted, running my hand through my hair.

"Well, shit," Maki said, taking a deep breath and letting his cheeks puff out.

"That's dangerous. He's become even more mad over the years since you ran. Obsessive doesn't begin to describe how he is now," Remi said as her hand shook in mine. Her skin turned deathly pale and Maki wrapped an arm around her shoulders.

"But it might work," Maki whispered to Remi.

Hope was there. I wanted to give them that hope that one day we could all go home and live a life free of that madman.

"I don't want anyone else I care about to die," Remi sniffled as tears formed in the corner of her scarred eyes. "So promise me, you won't do anything foolish. Well, anymore than this."

"I promise to try," I said with a reassuring grip on her hand. "We all know just what is at stake here, but this burning rage is finally able to do something about all our suffering. Lyron is giving us that chance to put an end to things."

We sat in silence before Maki looked back at me. "What does Lyron have to do with wanting Desmond dead? They have history?"

"Back at their previous Order, they were both soldiers and I don't know the details. Lyron just said that Desmond was kicked out for being too extreme."

"Gotcha. So, Desmond's been pissing people off all over. Makes sense." Crossing his arms, Maki nodded to himself.

I shook my head. "He does have that ability. If he wasn't so crazy, then maybe our people could have overthrown him. We were a people of peace, and he is a man of war. When I think about the inevitable that someone was bound to come eventually and destroy that, it just makes me feel so helpless. Like there was nothing we could have done differently."

Remi puffed out her cheeks in frustration. Something she did ever since she was little. "Because there was nothing," she grumbled. We watched in horror and disbelief as we let it happen. We were scared."

Sitting in silence, the roars of the fights were heavily muted but still made its way all the way to my room. Exhaling, I didn't want to dwell on what was done. We had a chance to right the wrongs of those who didn't know better and destroy the one who took our peace and shattered it into oblivion.

But first, there was a festival to get through. I found this Order full of oddities, but for once, I wanted to take part in the fun instead of just training to become better.

"Let's go down to watch the fights. I want to enjoy this moment before we prepare to go to war," I said, stretching my arms above my head before swinging them down to my sides.

"Oh, hell yeah!" Maki pumped his fist into the air. "That Lyron guy was amazing to watch, kind of hope he gets challenged more, but I doubt it after yesterday's little show."

Remi quirked the side of her mouth up. "That idiot should have left her alone. Lyron was simply showing him what happens when someone dares to disrespect his woman."

"Come on," I groaned. "Let's go before you make me puke."

Their laughter rang behind me and my heart swelled with warmth. I'd missed them so much over the years, and I thought I'd never see them again. Walking down the halls, we talked and laughed as if the years of being a Wild never happened. As if all those horrible moments of nearly embracing death and capture disappeared. If I was to die tomorrow, this would be enough.

Approaching the arena, I saw Thor speaking to Ivy, her back to us. His shoulders were tense, his jaw clenched. Ivy waved her hands dismissively before walking away, not noticing me at all. Thor glanced our way and shook his head before turning on his smile and sauntering over.

"Hey, you're looking a hell of a lot better there, bodyguard," he said, lightly punching me in the shoulder.

"Lucky break," I tittered, clearing my throat. "I take it you know Remi and Maki."

"In faces, but it's nice to know names." Thor ran his hand through his hair, sheepishly smiling.

Maki stared at me and Thor like I introduced the savior.

"You know him?" Maki whispered frantically.

"Yeah, this is Thor. I heard he had some refugees coming in. So I presumed you knew each other?"

"Maki is a little star struck," Remi clarified. "If it's the second in command named Thor, then he just met the guy who stopped the people coming after us."

"The one and only, I guess." I smirked at Thor as he turned a bright red.

"Glad I could help, really," Thor said. "Wish I could have helped sooner."

No doubt meaning Remi's eyes. Thor's expression softened, and Remi, as if sensing it, responded with a bright smile.

"It has its advantages. I can hear much better. Like hearts beating faster or pulses for lying. I listen better to influxes in tone when someone talks. The steps of someone trying to sneak up or someone I know. Everyone has a unique way of walking, like a unique code," she said, keeping count with her fingers. "The only downfall is hearing this idiot snore."

Maki blushed as he shushed at her. "Hey, I can't help I finally get good sleep here."

"Hey, that's what matters," Thor said to Maki, beaming a sincere smile. He took pride in what he did. Being a hero to those wanting to escape. "Are you coming to the arena? With all the refugees coming in, I'm sorry that we don't have time for tours. While everyone is busy, would you like an official one?"

"That would be nice," Remi agreed. "Maybe one day I can navigate the place without Maki helping me."

"One step at a time." Thor glanced at me expectantly. "Did you want to come with? I see you know them, so it's up to you or did you want to go watch the fights?"

"I'll go inside. Have fun," I said, waving them off.

Maki was over the moon, excited and blasted questions at Thor about the Order. Remi held onto her brother's arm and off they went.

Letting out a breath of air, I smiled before turning to go into the arena. The fights would continue until tomorrow, but from the sound of the cheers, I had nothing to worry about for once. I would worry about Desmond later. Today I just wanted to enjoy the moment.

CHAPTER 10 A TOUCH IN THE SHADOWS

<u>Milana</u>

"I can't believe this place is so huge," Remi gushed as we sat for dinner together.

Maki was busy still talking Thor's ear off a few tables down. Thor humored him and even invited him to become part of the scouts. Maki's questions made Thor even more enthusiastic. The dinner hall was packed beyond capacity and yet it didn't trigger my flight or fight response like before. I was at ease and the company of Remi certainly helped calm my nerves. I could feel Lyron's gaze from the front of the room. Every time I glanced at him, he was eyeing me intently.

"It takes a bit to get used to, but I'm sure you'll get there," I reassured her.

Kira remained out of sight as far as I could tell. A part of me worried, but most of me was smug about it. A part of me also wondered where Ivy was. Usually I couldn't get her away from me although her company was not always unwelcome. The burns on her back and on Remi's eyes reminded me just how much Desmond needed to fall.

"With you here, I feel better about it. Thor is keeping my brother busy." A knowing smile spread across her face as she leaned over to me, whispering intently. "And that's okay. Having him around me all the time was a little bothersome. Maybe I can stay in your room tonight?"

"Of course! We can talk about your adventures," I said, leaning in briefly before straightening.

"I'm more interested in your stories. Fighting off Desmond's men at every turn, avoiding capture, seducing the Leader here. You have kept busy."

"Who's seducing who?" Lyron said, appearing in front of us. I smiled weakly. Remi giggled as my face turned bright red.

"I was just teasing her. You see, she was always a bit of a shy one, especially around me, back when I knew her. However, fighting till blood is spilt is nothing completely new," Remi said.

"Hey, now. I didn't always draw blood," I pouted, going back to my meal.

"Only when they called you a boy," Remi sang as she poked my shoulder. "I'm staying with her tonight so I can jog her memory."

"Remi!" I swatted her arm, and she laughed with a tiny snort.

Brat.

"I may have to talk to you about these memories of yours. They seem very entertaining." Lyron smiled as he patted Remi's shoulder and walked away to leave the dining hall.

Remi's smile stayed on her face long after he walked away. "I like him. For you anyway."

Groaning, I continued my meal as I looked at Maki and Thor. Thor was less enthused now as he eyed me suspiciously. Maki got his attention again, and they continued talking. The thought of Thor being disappointed didn't bother me, but that he thought he had a claim to me did. If he had an issue, I'd rather he just come out and say it instead of sulking like a child.

"You look distracted." Remi's voice broke through my thoughts, touching her fingers to my forearm.

"Sorry, just thinking about something not important," I said as I took our plates. "I'll get rid of your plate and we can head back to my room. Tonight is the last day of the festival. I hear they sing and dance, maybe like home? Would you like to go?"

"That would be nice. It seems like you've been just training and not enjoying yourself, so I'm glad to be your partner. However, wouldn't you rather ask Lyron?" Arching an eyebrow, I knew exactly what she was insinuating.

"Nah, he told me he doesn't go to these things. Makes him feel uncomfortable, or something," I said with a shrug.

"Well, that's too bad for him, and good for me." Giggling, she waited for me to stand up. "Maki," she called out. "I'll be with Milana tonight, so don't worry about me."

"Got it," he called back.

Remi stood up slowly and swung her leg over the wooden bench at the table and stretched her hand to me. Extending my arm, she looped her arm in mine and we walked to the dining hall where used plates were taken. Dropping them off, we headed to the market.

The crowd was sparse outside the main entrance. Most of the noise seemed to come from the field just beyond the fortress. There were people gathering large branches, old broken furniture from the Order, and whatever else they could find. Three different piles of wooden debris were in a triangle, not too far away from each other, but far enough to not catch fire from the other. The space was enough for about fifty people to dance close together.

Many were laughing and enjoying themselves as we walked up the hill to the field. Kira was there, leading to the front. I could see this being her place as head of the community. Her lip was split and her eye was swollen, but I imagined more of the damage was in her ribs. She wasn't moving around too much, just telling others what to do.

"You tensed," Remi noted.

"Just saw the one who almost made me minced meat. She's organizing the people."

"Ah, sounds pleasant." Remi bumped me with her hip, urging me to move on. "I imagine questions will come about how you healed so fast."

"Probably."

"Then let's avoid them until night," Remi urged, turning us around. I smirked and didn't argue as we headed back down to the fortress.

No one had asked out loud yet, but I saw the suspicious looks. Perhaps I was hasty about using my abilities, but knowing that Lyron was aware of my abilities made me want to hide them less. When I first arrived, I would have hid them no matter the cost, but now I was growing comfortable.

I couldn't tell if comfort was good or bad yet, but I didn't want to live in fear. I wanted to blaze my own path.

After spending the rest of the afternoon in my room, we finally headed out at sunset. Less prying eyes, and more distractions now that the fires were lit. Illuminating the field, they were truly grand and inspiring to look at. The sparks floating up to the broken moon were a beacon to me. Putting me at ease, I felt at peace.

Maki was back with us as he guided his sister. Thor was going to evaluate him tomorrow to become a scout. He was going on about that, and I felt ill at ease, especially with Remi's condition. However, she encouraged him and her feelings felt sincere. Perhaps she felt guilty and wanted him to spread his wings. The way she brought it up earlier when we were in my room pointed to that. *I want him to be happy and live his own life.*

Perhaps if my brother was my protector, and he had a chance to do what he wanted in a place I felt safe, maybe at one point I would have thought the same.

"Hey!" I heard Ivy call out. "Sorry I was busy helping with the setup of tonight. The fights always make me nauseous. I saw how Kira came out, but you look good."

"Fast healer," I answered quickly, not offering more than that.

"Uh, huh," she said skeptically, before turning her head to the fires. "Well, I'll be around, but enjoy the music and dancing. I see you wore the green outfit I made you. Nice choice."

I smiled and said thank you as she turned and frolicked away. Honestly, she had a hard time sitting still, and this pace with Remi helped me get my bearings again. Before, Ivy kept me too busy with everything. Remi allowed me to enjoy what was happening around me. She reminded me to enjoy it, too.

"Green was always your color," Remi agreed, although Ivy was far away.

"Hey ladies, I heard the dances will be starting up soon. May I escort you?" Maki offered with a bright smile as he bounded up to us.

"I suppose. I hope it's close enough to the music and so I can feel the dances," Remi said as Maki assured her he did his best. Maki took her arm and Remi transferred over. Her stick was in my room because she was afraid people would trip over it. While I had many issues with relying on others, she was grateful we could help her. *It's hard when your world is taken away and suddenly the rest of your senses are heightened. Takes a bit to get used to, but I'm learning to adjust.*

Adjusting was hard. A lot of that has been going around lately.

When Maki brought us to a spot by Thor, I almost rolled my eyes. Of course, he would be next to a person I wanted to avoid. I had no issues with the man until he came back from his mission. I was even patient enough to not hunt down the prisoner. The least he could do was not be so pitiful.

"Hey Remi, hey Milana," Thor called out as he waved, unbothered.

"Keeping my brother busy, I see," Remi said with a smile.

"More like keeping me busy. Does he always ask so many questions?" Thor asked in a whisper to tease Maki. Maki's face turned red.

"Only when he's been invited to. You did it to yourself." Remi smiled as she nodded her head quickly, as if saying *that was that, no debate allowed.*

"Ha, I'll keep that in mind," Thor muttered as he hit Maki on the shoulder with a smile.

Watching the dancers was bringing me back to my childhood. So many nights, I watched my mother dance with her friends and laugh the night away. Young women, older women, elderly women all had a different dance, symbolizing the stages of life and womanhood. The men had their own dances, couples had dances, children had dances. I missed them all.

As I was lost in my thoughts, I saw Lyron from the corner of my eye. He was a short distance away, but watchful. He didn't seem to be watching me though, as if lost in thought himself. However, he glanced at me, and his eyes widened. Standing up, I excused myself and followed him. Lyron made no dash to run but didn't make it easy to catch up.

Widening my stride, I went into a slow jog as I passed through the entrance to the fortress. I saw his shadow from the torches around the corner of a corridor. The only sound was our footsteps as mostly everyone was enjoying the festivities.

Rounding the corner, I ran into his chest as he stood there with his arms crossed.

Rubbing my nose, the sting was sudden but hardly something to complain about. "Could have been a couple paces back, geez."

"Why did you follow me?" he asked, narrowing his eyes.

"Because you told me you didn't go to these things, so I wanted to know why."

"No reason," he said, running a hand through his hair, and averted his gaze.

We stood together in silence, neither of us feeling welcome, and yet unwilling to go. I cleared my throat to break the silence. "It's a beautiful night. The clouds are gone, and it's as if the sparks are reaching out to join the stars," I murmured softly. I found myself mesmerized by the view for quite some time. Maybe it was the Firan in me, but I took pleasure in watching the flames and sparks dance.

"The flames are beautiful, but like all beautiful things, we can't truly possess them," he said, his eyes softening as he leaned over at me. I took a step back, my back meeting the cool stone wall. His arms formed a cage around me, and he grimaced, looking away.

My heart raced, wanting him to do something and yet afraid he would. Oak's words from earlier made sense, the same with Sunny's.

"My mother told me that if you want something, you pick it. You will have it, but it will die. If you..." I paused. "Love something, you will let it grow and flourish where it belongs."

"Your mother was a wise woman," he said, a corner of his mouth curved into a brief smile.

Silence stretched once more, and I could feel his breath against my skin. The air between us grew thicker as he leaned in closer.

"You were never meant to be mine," Lyron whispered. His voice in anguish.

"I am no one's to claim," I whispered as his forehead touched mine.

A million moments passed in our silence. His hand reached for mine, while his other hand supported his weight against the wall above me.

"You should go. Remi will be missing you," he said and started to lean away.

"I'll go when I want," I challenged, gripping his hand. "You say I was never meant to be yours? Is that because you're afraid I'll reject you if you asked me?"

His eyes blazed with a dark hunger, normally concealed behind an apathetic mask. Seeing this side of him thrilled a part of me. "Damn you, woman," he gritted out, pulling me toward him and crashing our lips together.

My self control snapped. I gasped into his mouth as deepened the kiss. His tongue danced with mine. I felt clumsy with my head, trying to keep up with my body.

A quiet moan left my mouth as every bit of tension floated away. Air circulated around us like a small breeze before dying off. The heat was too much, and yet I wanted more. His hands gripped the hair at the base of my neck, holding me in place as my lips moved in rhythm with his. My hands were holding onto his forearms, not knowing where to go but just wanting to hold him somehow.

Suddenly, he backed away. A chill sweeping through the warmth.

"I won't take a woman who will not have me," he said, catching his breath. He slowly turned and walked away down the hall.

I processed his words for a moment, keeping my back to the wall for stability. I had been kissed before, but never like that. Never as if I was the air he breathed and the only thing anchoring him to this world. Breathing in and out deeply, I let my heart rate slow down. Coming back to my senses, I cleared my throat and turned to walk back to Remi, Maki, and Thor.

"So, what caught your attention?" Thor said, coming out from behind the archway at the entrance as I passed him, making me jump back.

My heart pounded for a whole different reason.

"Don't do that!" I said as I put my hand on my chest.

He waited for me to catch my breath. I almost forgot he was a scout. Supposed to be hard to detect and hidden when he wanted to be.

"Well?" he asked as we stood there.

I narrowed my eyes at him and shook my head. "The hell do you care? You've been against everything else I've been doing since you came back. Didn't wait for someone to save me, so I fought and suddenly I'm a disappointment to you," I said through gritted teeth.

He stared at me blankly, then shook his head. "I was worried about you. Lyron, while he's our Leader, didn't need to have you fight Kira. That was dangerous. All of that was dangerous. Did you know she could have killed you? There's a reason she is cocky. She can back it up. You are a Wild who fought to survive, not striving for strategy. Watching you become her punching bag was far from enjoyable for me."

I scoffed. My hands felt hot and my blood boiled. "I didn't need to be saved. She crossed the line when Lyron was trying to help me. I am not a woman that needs to be told where to go, what to say, or how to defend myself by any man. Lyron understands that perfectly well, and yet somehow it passes over your head as you play hero to the Order."

"I play hero, sure. But at least I'm not some twisted Wild who ran, while others got hurt because they couldn't face their fears. Ivy and Remi got hurt because of you," he said, then grimaced.

He hit a nerve so deep that I stood there in silence.

I backed away from him. He was right. I was a monster, even if he hadn't said it. The agony of the weakness I allowed to let me run, the strength I only just started to have confidence in, the heat of a kiss and the chill of rejection. It was all too much for the moment, and then Thor's jab straight to my regret in life was the wrong move for him. My movements happened so fast I hardly remember them.

My fist collided with his jaw with a solid *thunk*. My knuckles stung, but the satisfaction of watching him recoil with surprise was worth it.

"Feel like a man, now? So much for a hero. I messed up back then. I know it. Save your hero shit for them, I'm over it," I said, turned, and walked back to my room.

Thor did not follow, but I felt we were being watched. Looking around, I saw Maki peek behind the corner. He didn't follow either, but I presumed he worried where I had gone off to.

"Go back to Remi, just tell her I was tired," was all I said as I kept walking up the stairs.

I was done running.

CHAPTER 11 DANCING FLAME

<u>Milana</u>

Lyron owed me for this. Not that the fool needed a bodyguard. In fact, his raw strength outweighed mine by a ridiculous amount in training, but something told me it was to keep an eye on me. His demeanor always seemed awkward, educated compared to many of us who only knew survival. The last few days since our 'kiss' he hadn't made any other advances, and we haven't spoken a word of it to each other. As if it was a dream. Our training continued now that the festival was completed and most had gone home to their own Orders. However, some stuck around like Tank. I remembered him saying yesterday at dinner he found the love of his life although it seemed she was uninterested. Oddly enough, he kept his eye on me. Rolling my eyes in response, the others giggled.

Thor kept his distance, his jaw black and blue, which gave me great joy. This was the only Order that I had fought all three members of leadership and still was welcomed.

Leaning against the rough rock pillar, I watched from a safe distance as the citizens of Eagle Point Order approached him for the weekly update on crops, water supply, and other mundane hemming and hawing. This entire fortress was built from rock, most likely limestone, and I had the chance to count every block on all the pillars. One hundred and twenty-six. My count had been verified twice. Now moving onto the east wall, I was nearing three hundred when I heard Lyron clearing his throat.

"You seem preoccupied. Is something more important than guarding me?" A smile crossed his face as he leaned over the armrest of his chair, resting his jaw on his knuckles.

Scoffing at the idea I could be anything other than bored, I turned my nose up at him and crossed my arms. "If I set you on fire, that would entertain me enough to pay attention," I said.

His laugh echoed through the large stone room. The sound was rare from him, and it drew my gaze. To see him at ease was even more rare. Always at attention, seeing threats in everyone and yet he led this Order with grace and fairness. Most leaders were devils in disguise, the lust for power overcoming their reason. Lyron was far from that kind of person. Where Thor was the hero of the Order, Lyron was willing to do what had to be done, no matter the cost.

"And here I thought you didn't hate me, Milana."

Damn him for saying my name like that. The way he said it bothered me, like he enjoyed the way it rolled off his tongue. It felt too familiar and personal and my cheeks flushed something fierce. I preferred the title of Wild, one that I was slowly losing. Kept me at a distance and them too. However, the slow ease into life here didn't allude me. I had found a home.

"I don't hate you. I just find this job more annoying by the day," I said.

Lyron stood up and approached me. Averting my gaze, I stood up straight. Uncrossing my arms, I resorted to putting them on my hips. His arms mimicked mine as he cocked his head to the side. His thoughts were lost on me. Reading him was impossible at the best of most moments. Guarding him was difficult since he enjoyed being elusive.

"Well, I suppose we could go on a scouting mission. Wouldn't want you bored and setting me on fire. I'll save my curiosity about your fire control for another day." He smiled as I checked to make sure no one was around. Casually mentioning my fire abilities now that I was near him most days still made me uneasy.

"You really need your brain checked. I could engulf you or just send a spark over, up to you, but right now I'm very tempted to engulf that ego of yours. It wouldn't hurt for it to be knocked down a peg." I started walking to the exit.

I could hear his calm footsteps behind me as I tried to be quick with mine. He was so much taller than me that it was hard for me to keep a lead or follow, but right now my pride didn't want to follow.

"Be that as it may, I am curious how you could hide it so well. Those who can control elements often lose control with their emotions," he continued. His line of conversation was often held in contempt with most who could control elements. I just had to get used to it. Offense wasn't his goal, but he was annoying.

I could feel the snap in my brain as I turned around. My finger pointed to him as a string of fire erupted from the tip. The line stopped just as it reached his shirt. His face looked to me in surprise, glanced down to touch his chest, and back up to me in glee.

"Seriously, you have no boundaries with these things, do you? I sometimes wonder if you're just a boy in a man's body when you're this annoying and insensitive," I said, jabbing my finger into his chest where the fire would have hit him.

"My apologies. Curiosity and all," he said, putting his hands up in surrender.

"Forgiven. Now let's go before I really decide to set you on fire," I said, turning around and walking through the entrance.

"That's not nice."

"You're the one who wanted me as a guard. Now let's go already."

We walked to the border and kept along the perimeter. Lately, the commotion had been kept to a minimum. Thor's men had a few new recruits, so they were busy training and ran extra routes to make sure the quiet stayed that day. Even the news of the prisoner was kept silent. I didn't pry like I had been asked to. However, I didn't know if it was out of fear. Reaching for the past was hurtful. It brought back memories I'd rather forget. And realizing the impact of my actions on Ivy and Remi. As much as Thor was right, I didn't want to be that scared girl anymore.

"You're lost in thought again," Lyron said as he held a low branch to the side for me.

"I tend to when I'm out in nature. Remember this used to be home for me? Or not here specifically, but around here," I clarified as he raised an eyebrow.

Silence spread between us and I imagined this would be far less awkward if I didn't constantly remember the way his body commanded mine when we kissed. I thought I had experienced most feelings: hope, dread, passion, and sorrow. My heart had raced in the heat of battle, pounded while I fled for my life, and frozen in horror at the sight of my family's lifeless bodies. When he kissed me, my heart sang. Whether it was a song to lead me to ruin or otherwise was still in the air.

"I thought you would have avoided the forest after what you had gone through," he pondered.

One might expect me to avoid vast, open spaces, and for the most part, I did just that. The forest, on the other hand, offered me a sanctuary where I could tune into the gentle rustling of the grass, the shifting winds, the symphony of woodland creatures, and the subtle cues they provided when danger lurked nearby.

While most would find it a threat, I found it a safeguard. The times I was nearly captured were in the abandoned cities. The ruins that lined the crumbling concrete roads. I avoided those open areas only to find solace in the forests. Which was why I was so close to Eagle Point Order when I first met Lyron.

"I never had issues with forests. In fact, it has brought me to my most interesting adventure," I countered as I jogged a few paces ahead of him, hearing a nearby stream.

He didn't question my words, simply watched as I took a drink from the clear water. Cool and refreshing, it eased my thirst and I let out a breath of air. Eagle Point Order was settled by a natural spring. The water was always cool and easy to work with. But fresh from the forest was like a moment of bliss.

"Are you happy?" Lyron asked, his breath hitching.

I stood up straight and wiped my mouth with the back of my hand. "I'm not unhappy."

"If I asked you to stay, would you?"

I eyed him suspiciously since we had this conversation before. There was a plea in his voice. Taking in a deep breath, I looked at the moon in the blue sky.

"I said I would stay to have a chance at killing Desmond. What more do you want me to say?"

He stood before me. "Damn stubborn is what you are," he scoffed, shaking his head, then he walked away.

Following him, my throat felt like it was on fire. The cool water was useless now. "What the hell do you want from me? You make me your bodyguard, kiss me, train me, talk like a friend—what am I supposed to do with that?" I asked, throwing my hands up.

Lyron stopped and turned on his heel, and I nearly collided with him. "Is Desmond all you think about? That prisoner had much to say about your relationship with him."

Acid through my veins spread like wildfire. I panted for a moment as Lyron turned to walk away. I briefly remember him mumbling something before I anchored myself with one leg and swung the other to strike at him. He dodged and took a fighting stance.

"Come again?" I swung my punches yelling, "I only had one relationship with that monster - to get away and kill him."

Lyron's stance only took the defensive, which only heightened my anger.

"So, you never spread your legs for him? Gave him a taste? It would explain why he's so desperate to have you." He didn't have the chance to continue as I landed a blow to his gut, knocking him to the ground.

"You seem very interested in what my legs have been doing, but I'll humor you." I kneeled and watched him squirm for air before recovering. "The only thing he had ever spread on me was my parent's blood. The splatter from their throats as he sliced them in front of me." I stood up and spit on the ground before him. "Next time you want to be a possessive asshole, talk to Kira. I'm not interested."

I left him there, on the ground as I jogged back to the Order. I worked off the steam along the way. My knuckles were bloodied from a tree who was at the wrong place at the wrong time. No one approached me and I was given a wide girth. Even Maki was quiet.

Back in my room, I screamed into my bed. I had Thor mad at me and Lyron, acting like a foolish boy. One that kissed me, the other accusing me. Without Remi and Ivy, I would have left immediately. After the festival, it had been interesting to see Ivy join our little group. Ivy would let Remi feel the fabrics and choose what felt the most comfortable. Just like how I was made to feel like a new woman, Remi had a new wardrobe. I was grateful for Ivy's hospitality, and I was happy Remi made another friend.

Dinner that night was quiet. Maki had gone with Thor and Lyron on a scouting mission. Remi and Ivy kept each other well socialized as I fumed over Lyron's words. They crept into my mind and made my skin crawl. The thought of being with Desmond sickened me.

I woke up in a sweat that night. The nightmare made me relive the fear and horror as he made me watch my parents die and every time I fell asleep, I dreaded that he'd wake me only to kill me. He was a mountain lion that played with his food and I was his 'mouse' as he so affectionately called me.

Leaning over my bed, I vomited on the floor. Remembering how he would pet my cheek had set me off over the edge. I wish I could kill him a million times over in a million ways to erase him. His words and his touch needed to be evacuated from my skin and memory. But then Lyron's words would ring through my head and I wondered... *would he ever leave me in peace, even after death?*

Sleep alluded me. An uneasiness stirred and had me on alert. Something was wrong. Getting up, I quietly opened my door, aware of any sound. But there wasn't any. In the darkness of night, it would make sense, but this was too quiet. Many of the men were gone with Thor and Lyron. Kira was here and despite our issues, I had to find her. She knew this place like the back of her hand.

I found her room and opened the door silently despite the resistance of the wood against the metal of the hinge. Putting my hand on her mouth, she gasped and her eyes opened in fear. I put my finger to my mouth and waited until her breathing steadied.

"What the hell are you doing?" Kira whispered as she looked behind me.

"There's something wrong. I need you to get the women and children out of harm's way. Can you do that without being seen?" My eyes pleaded with her as she twisted her face in confusion.

"Yeah, uh huh, you're being paranoid," she scoffed before moving to roll over in bed and go back to sleep.

"And if I'm not?" I urged, grabbing her shoulder. She tensed and then let out a breath.

"I hope you're wrong about this," she said, getting out of bed. "Leave it to me. Report back to me with any findings. We will be in the medical ward. There's a door that can be barricaded from the inside only."

"Get there and stay there. I have a feeling it'll be a long night. No matter what you hear."

"I don't understand," Kira groaned as I opened her door.

"You don't have to yet. I'm hoping I'm wrong," I said before sneaking down the hall.

Feeling less worried about the others, I made my way up past my room and to the rooftop. There was a vantage point Thor's men would guard, where I could see for miles. Tonight there was only one man left behind to guard and the torch they had was no longer lit. I closed my eyes and put my hand to the stone at my feet. Nothing.

Slowly creeping around, I looked to the edge and saw what I feared. A body of a man, limp against the stone barricade around the edge. Blood pooled on the stone, and I quickly made my way back to my room. I retrieved my dual blades from their resting place beneath my bed and fastened them securely to my waist, using their harness. Swiftly, I crisscrossed them behind me within their sheaths. Taking in a deep breath, I let it out slowly. A shiver coursed through me, causing the hairs on the back of my neck to stand on end.

Down the corridors, I swiftly moved, sometimes hearing distant 'shushes' from women and children. Wherever the intruders were, they were keeping busy. Perhaps working from the outside in. Heading towards the entrance, my eyes caught movement.

"Ah, the Firan bitch is here, after all. Desmond has been looking for you, mouse," a man named Rivers called out. He was tall, built like a fortress, and cruel. Short black hair, dark brown eyes, and darkened skin from the sun.

"This Firan bitch may just have a few things to tell Desmond if he was brave enough to come here himself.

Looks like you're his bitch more than I ever was," I taunted as he charged at me. Taking one of my blades, I aimed it at him and he stopped. "Now, why are you here?"

Seeing movement from my left, I dodged the brunt of the blow. A blade nicked my shoulder, and the blood was minimal. I went a few paces back and looked around to see if there was anyone else close by. The one who charged me I didn't recognize but was shorter and lankier with light colored hair. He cursed as he stood behind Rivers.

"This is the one Desmond wants alive. Everyone else can die," Rivers said, and I grimaced.

I was seething with rage. If they thought I was going down quietly, they had another thing coming. "The bastard can come here himself if he wants to see me alive. I'll sooner slit my throat than be dragged back to him like a dog."

"That can be arranged. He said he preferred you alive. It wasn't a full requirement," the man behind Rivers said with a twisted smile.

I struggled to contain the flames that sprouted from my arm, their fiery tendrils swirling towards the man and searing through his shirt, scorching his chest while emitting a piercing scream.

I raised my eyebrow as he cried out in agony. Served him right. I looked to Rivers, who charged me again. Using my flame, I created a whip where I lashed into his arm. He grimaced, and his eyes turned to me with murderous intent.

From behind me, I heard the faint yell of a man, "We found them!"

My blood ran cold as my fire calmed down. Looking back, I ran full speed. I didn't see a woman in the halls, but there were the sounds of a forceful entry as the echoes radiated through the halls to the medical unit.

"Hey, boys," I called out to the five of them. "Your fight is with me."

I seized both my blades, and my flames enveloped them. I charged towards them, one blade slashing while the other defended. One went down quickly as his stomach was slashed open. Another's throat was cut and blood coated the walls. I hoped that Kira was able to bring everyone to safety, and that they were kept out of harm's way. This may not have started as my home, but I'd be caught dead if I didn't defend it.

Rivers and his companion joined in, taking me from behind in a headlock. I twisted my body and bit into River's arm. His hold loosened ever so slightly and he head butted me in the back of my skull. Warmth oozed down my neck. Breaking skin wouldn't deter me, but it certainly made fighting harder when seeing straight was no longer working. I concentrated my will to intensify the flames, expanding their range of destruction and leaving no room for error.

"I didn't think you had it in you, Milana," Rivers said as three of his men's blood soaked the ground.

"No? Well, I love to disappoint you." Breathing heavily, I smiled although my body ached. I had many cuts and bruises from their attacks and compared to Kira, they were nothing, but they were still seven against one—now four against one.

"Cocky bitch."

They encircled me. None of them were Firans, and my stamina was dwindling. Lyron was not expected to return soon with Thor. Kira was safeguarding the women; it was up to me to bring this to an end.

I yelled as I put all my strength into a wall of flame that roared to life. The smell of their burning flesh made my stomach churn as they collapsed before me. The walls were charred black, and I fell to the ground on my knees. I gasped for air when I saw a man come around the corner only to run. Coward. I would make sure no one made it back to Desmond.

I found the strength to stand and ran after him. My legs were in agony, every movement felt like my last, my lungs felt like they were going to explode. I chased after him into the forest. He tripped on a root ahead of me. He whimpered as he looked back at me, horrified. "Have mercy! He made me do it! I had no choice," he pleaded as he backed up into a tree and covered his face with his hands.

"Tell me why you came," I demanded, the strength in my voice surprising me.

"Desmond demanded that we bring back the prisoner and make sure you come back to him. He didn't tell us you were a Firan. How is this possible?" he cried out.

"Make sure I come back to him," I repeated and laughed. "I may be a freak of a Firan, a woman, but I will never go back to him. I will not be his mouse. If he wants me, he can come here to claim me. Anything else deems him a coward. But I suppose it's pointless to tell you this, since you'll be dead soon."

"I have a family at home. I didn't kill anyone," he begged, and I looked him over.

My body swayed and my vision doubled. I used too much of my flame and the small cuts were adding up. I believed him and was too tired to follow through with my threat.

"Consider yourself dead," I said, barely keeping myself standing. "I suggest you take your family and run from the Desert Order. This is the only warning I will give you. The next time I see you here under his orders, I will kill you."

He ran without a word of thanks, but I didn't expect it. Falling to my knees, I collapsed on the ground.

Darkness took me.

I heard men yelling during my sleep. A nightmare, perhaps? Maybe Desmond killed me. I'd hoped when I died I'd see my family again. But there was nothing. Perhaps I didn't deserve their presence. Perhaps they were in hell waiting for me.

I remembered warmth brushing against my face.

I heard Remi. "Let her rest."

Remi. I wanted to reach out to make sure she was safe, but my body refused.

Lyron's voice grated nearby. "It's been a week."

"She used too much power... give her time."

Silence stretched forever. Voices would come to me here and there. Remi's was the most common.

Thor's voice came to me, too. "I'm sorry. Please come back so we can talk like we used to."

I wanted to. I never wanted to fight. I never wanted to cause others pain.

"I made you a new outfit for when you wake up. I think you'll like it. It's red," Ivy sniffled as I felt a hand grasp mine.

Darkness swirled around me. Time ticked at an immeasurable pace. Worried whispers around me broke through the darkness at times, but I didn't know how long between.

A memory came to me after the darkness and voices. My mother was standing in the kitchen and I was humming to myself as I cleaned the floor with a tiny broom.

"*Madra*," I called to her. "Do you think we go to the moon when we die? Won't the moon run out of room?"

"Oh my darling, the moon is a special place. The moon goddess accepts all and makes room for us in her embrace."

"What if she thinks I'm a freak?"

"Your flame is a gift, darling. Once you are ready to embrace it, the world will never be ready. I believe the moon goddess gave you this gift to protect something. What that is, you'll have to find out."

I gasped for air as my eyes opened.

Chapter 12 Brutal Sins

<u>Milana</u>

My body ached.

I was alone in a room I faintly remembered. Glancing to the side of me, I saw Lyron sleeping in a chair and I recognized his scattered papers. How long was I asleep for? Felt like I had slept for a lifetime and yet not at all. My limbs were heavy, even my skull felt like lead as I tilted to see Lyron better. He looked haggard, the usual sheen in his air looked dull, and there were bags under his eyes even as he rested.

The sunshine peeked through the balcony archway, the dust in the air glimmering in the rays. Morning songbirds chirped eagerly outside. Tiling my head to the balcony, I saw a few of them perched on the rail. Half of me wondered if I was dead. This felt too peaceful and quiet to be a moment in my life. It took me back to the days where I was a Wild, waking up to the sounds of birds and watching the sun rise.

Hearing a clutter from where Lyron was, I tilted my head only to see his eyes widened with shock. Walking to me with trepidation, as if I may disappear from his sight.

"You're awake," he stated in wonder. His jaw quivered.

"Was I dead?" I asked, my voice raspy. Coughing, he grabbed a pitcher of water and poured into a cup that was on the bedside table. I reached for it, but he ignored it and put the cup to my lips as he tenderly helped me sit up enough to swallow.

He spoke so gently, it was as if talking to one of the children. I never thought of Lyron having a soothing voice, but in this moment he eased my mind. "Nearly. We found you in the woods when we came back after Kira sent the warning call that the Order was under attack."

I smiled and a breath of air huffed out in a sad attempt at a laugh. "I thought you'd leave me there for dead after what happened the day you left."

His lips curved into a smile and he let my head down gently to the pillow. "No such luck for you. Apparently, after Kira was sure there was no other threat, she saw the burns to the walls and the corpses. She kept the people in the medical wing for a time, but then when she checked to see the coast was clear, she was able to send the message.

"By the time we came back, day had broken, and no one knew where you were. I found a man blathering about fire hidden on the outskirts of the Order, and he told us where he had approached a woman like the grim reaper. I could only presume he meant you. I think you scared him for life. We found you barely breathing, but your body was still warm. Too warm, so we brought you back here, and Ivy gave you an ice bath and patched you up."

He paused, his gaze fixed on me, and then he sat on the bed, placing a gentle hand on mine and holding it firmly. "You saved this Order. I reacted harshly when I heard about Desmond's men coming and I thought I could intercept them. The information was incorrect and as a result, we almost lost everything had you not been strong enough to face them. You saved everyone, and no matter what the others think or believe, I owe you everything. Anything you wish, it shall be done. That is my vow to you."

My face flushed with heat. I had never heard a proclamation of a vow, and the wave of both gratitude and unease filled me. Through everything, I had believed I would never have a home again. However, at this moment I felt a bond with not only Lyron but the people in it. Even if they saw me as a monster, even if I did wrong, I wanted to protect them. I wanted to make sure that this Order didn't become like the Desert Order.

"My wish is to end, Desmond. To end this fear, to make it so people stop running from their homes. I want him to die," I whispered as I closed my eyes and thought of a life full of sunshine and laughter.

"It shall be done. You have my word. I'll let Remi know you are awake. It's been ten days, and she only left last night after Maki dragged her away," he said as he stood up and walked to the door. "Rest up and when you feel ready, we can let you stretch your legs again."

"Let me, my ass," I muttered as he shook his head. "I'll get up myself."

"I expected nothing less," he muttered before closing the door behind him, a smirk plastered on his face with a twinkle in his eyes.

I smiled as I slowly sat up. The ache of my muscles was excruciating, as if my body had been stabbed a thousand times. Judging from the bandages that I could see now that the blanket fell to my lap—maybe that wasn't too far off. Much of my body was wrapped up. My ribs, arms, legs, even my feet were wound securely with padding. The back of my head was tender, but it did not feel crusty from dried blood.

The door burst open as Remi tore in with Maki close behind her, tearing up when he saw me.

"I thought you'd never wake up. Why did you fight them alone?" she sobbed, collapsing on the bed so her head was on my legs. Although she landed on a cut, I didn't have the heart to tell her that the impact hurt. I rubbed her hair and let her cry it out.

After she gained her composure, she continued, "Kira led us deep into the halls. It was cold and when they tried to barge through the door, we wondered if this was the end. Then I heard you out there and Kira told us to stay where we were and that we had to keep quiet. She told me we had to trust you. She had killed a few on the way as she led us there, but the rest was in your hands since it was her duty to make sure we were taken care of so long as you held the front."

Kira had trusted me.

Initially, I had thought she was simply doing what needed to be done, but her trust extended beyond that. She trusted me enough to communicate to the women that while she protected them behind the door, I would stand guard in front of it. A strange surge of emotion welled up within me, perhaps pride. Yet, it was different from my usual experience of pride. Nonetheless, it didn't feel unfamiliar. The last time I recalled feeling this way was when my mother assured me that I would always have a home, even if I found someone and ventured out to forge my own path as a woman.

I finally had a home.

Thor came in and smiled. "Hey sleepy head. I heard you had a wild night. Kicking ass, taking names."

"Something like that," I said, remembering his words in my sleep as he walked to the bed.

"Good to see you awake. We made the perimeter more secure. Because of you, more men are joining the scouts. The reality is setting in that this could be all out war with the Desert Order soon."

"I don't want anyone to get hurt like the man did on the lookout point," I said with determination.

"Neither do we, so let's work hard together." He reached out his hand for mine. I brought my hand to his, and we shook.

Remi looked at both of us and smiled. "Let's let her rest," she said, sniffling as she pushed Thor out of the room. "If I hear you so much as breathe in her direction about working hard..." she chastised Thor as they walked down the hall and shut the door.

I smiled and shook my head. Somehow this felt exactly how it should be, friends and family in a place to call home. Although I had no blood relatives left, I still remembered the feeling I had as a child of security. For years, it was buried. I felt empowered by it. I had to gain my strength back, for not only myself but them too.

Days went by, and I gradually regained most of my strength, allowing me to return to lower-intensity training. The amount of fire I had conjured during the recent battle had exceeded any previous effort. Remi explained how the other Firans would succumb to exhaustion as Desmond pushed them to overexertion. Then, he began to experiment.

Fire, he pointed out, emanated from within us, yet we channeled it without a physical medium. Terrans had the earth at their disposal, while Aquans had bodies of water.

I contemplated the concept of taking a flame that didn't exist and willing it into being. Remi noted that even most Firans required an existing flame as a catalyst to assist with their abilities.

Maybe I was a monster.

It wasn't until a couple of weeks later that Lyron approached me with a sullen face. His face looked sunken in, like he hadn't slept for days. Coming to give my report on the perimeter check I worked with Oak on, I had just caught him leaving his room.

"You look rough," I said, reaching up to touch his cheek before realizing what I was doing and quickly withdrew my hand.

"That would be correct. The prisoner is finally ready to talk, but..."

"But, what? This is good news, right?" I said, confused. This was a victory.

His words spat out in aggravation. "He wants to make sure that he has an audience with the refugees. Particularly, you and Remi."

I kept my posture tall and proud, even though I hated this idea. "Well, I can talk to Remi and Maki, but I know she wants this to end just as much as me."

"If he dares to say a single thing to offend you, tell me and I will kill him where he stands," Lyron said, taking my shoulders, facing me with such dedication to his words. My faced blushed a bright red as I tried to look away. I didn't always know how to fully trust his words. Men had often been a source of problems in my life, so when Lyron offered a solution, I hesitated to seize the opportunity.

However, the idea of someone needing to kill on my behalf was a strange notion, considering I did just burn four men alive a month ago. "I think I can kill him myself should he offend me."

His smile was genuinely bright and pleased. "There's the fighter in you. I'd look forward to seeing that. He's very obnoxious."

"Consider it done Lyron," I said. Suddenly, a slight breeze stirred, which was odd since there shouldn't have been any drafts in the hallway by his room, devoid of windows. His eyes darkened, and he blinked a few times before averting his gaze.

"I'll be going to prepare the hall where I take the reports from the people. I will arrange with Thor to keep a perimeter and you talk to Remi and the others. We will finish this tonight and be done with it," he said as he hurried past me.

The switch in mood left me confused. Sunny and Oak told me he felt more for me than he did others. I didn't believe it then, but I wondered. Sunny was busy with Kira, refortifying rations and any unstable sections that needed fixing in case the worst should happen. Ivy was busy with them as well. Remi was my main company, along with the men on Thor's scouting team. I led some of the perimeter checks, but most kept a wide distance from me. I expected it after burning Desmond's men alive. No one mentioned my powers directly, but I did see a few of the refugees look at me with pride in their eyes. And fear.

Walking to Remi's room, I saw Kira ahead of me.

"I'm glad to see you're doing better. I didn't get to say thank you for the wake up call. It could have been bad here," she said, running her hand through her golden hair.

"I did what anyone would have done."

"Still, we owe you our lives. Takes a lot of courage to fight alone," she said, and smiled before patting my shoulder and continuing to her destination.

Everything was coming together quickly. The men were charged with monitoring the surrounding land and never on look out alone. They had a memorial for their fallen comrade while I was resting, and a memorial that I saw some visit frequently. Just a simple stack of rocks with a sword wedged in them. While I didn't know him personally, he still had a family. A family who wanted to see him grow old and live a happy life. He deserved more than a knife to the back in the dead of night. His death would not be in vain.

"Have you thought about what I said?" I heard Tucker say next to me as I watched people visit the man's small memorial.

"About revenge and justice?" I asked, knowing full well both still weighed heavily on my mind.

"And? What's your choice?"

"I think that man deserved better than the death he got. I think it's time this ended. I still may not know which one will win out, but I'm hoping his death won't be in vain." My hands formed fists at my sides as I looked at Tucker, who nodded before turning around to leave.

"I think when the time comes, you'll make the right choice," he said as he waved, walking away.

I could only hope so.

The night approached quickly, and Remi had decided to join me. Some of the refugee men remained further back, watching cautiously. Thor escorted the prisoner to where Lyron occupied his stone throne, a seat he reserved for formal audiences with the general populace or visiting leaders from other Orders. It was a tactic to project an aura of supremacy, a notion that had once struck me as silly when he explained it. Now, however, it made perfect sense. The commanding presence it exuded was undeniably intimidating, even to someone like me, who had long ceased to find Lyron intimidating in other ways.

"You are here today to answer for your crimes and to tell us about Desmond's plans. You asked for an audience, although I doubt it'll have the effect you think it will. They are here by choice and not under your tyrannical rule anymore." Lyron's voice left little room for debate. The absolution was strange after so long. But then he talked to me that way the first day or two that I was in his prison. Same as this man, although this man had been imprisoned for over a month. Omar was his name. He was filthy, bloodied, and smelled foul. His stench radiated through the room.

He smiled a crooked smile, looking around until his eyes found mine. "My crimes? I only did as I was told." He glanced to Remi and his smile twisted into a larger grin. "Ah, I remember those eyes. I remember what they used to be." Remi trembled as she curled into my side, as if trying to disappear. "*Be strong*," I whispered under my breath as I wrapped an arm around her waist.

His eyes went to me and his head tilted. "Ah, the mouse that escaped the trap. The desert trap that caught the rat. We forgot to shrink the trap after your brother was killed, defying our great Desmond. We should have taken and beaten you down. Trained you to be a doting wife, punished you severely for being part of that heinous family. I took great joy in killing them all. I took great joy in burning your parent's bodies after their blood painted the streets. Kept them hung for days until their bodies swelled. The smell was awful, but the message was loud and clear. Tell me, Milana, do you want death? Desmond will give it to you. Anything you want if you simply give him your powers. He's coming for you. What happened before was just the beginning. He will never stop coming for you."

It took all of me to keep from lashing out—tear him limb from limb. Lyron and Thor looked to me and thankfully I was able to breathe deeply, keeping my flame in check. "I didn't want these powers to begin with. Even if I could give them away, I would rather die here and now than give that bastard anything."

"Ah, but he said he wanted you to be his whore. To scream under him in pleasure, or pain. Your friend died that way, he tore her apart with his bare hands as he imagined you under him instead of her. Imagine dying and not even your own name is said. The last wife he took before you ran away."

My blood ran cold. Desmond was insane, but I didn't know the full severity until now. My anger boiled over until one of my fists lit a flame. He looked at my fist and to me and the smile turned into a puzzled frown.

"Did you think I wouldn't know what he wanted? His toyful glances, his touches that lingered too long on my skin. The night he stole our home was the day I swore I would never follow him. You're a foul little snake who fed on mice like me and all the women. Hurt my friends, killed my friends. Killed my brother."

He tried to speak, but I covered his mouth and screamed in his face. "I'm not finished, Omar!"

Clearing my throat, I took my hand from his mouth as the blood ran from his face. Pale as a ghost, I left him sitting there and walked over to Lyron. An unexpected strength surged within me as I noticed a dagger on his hip, snug in its holster. I met his gaze and then gestured to the dagger. He allowed me to move my hands toward it, and I took it from him. The way his eyes dilated left me unable to interpret their meaning, but in that moment, I felt like the most powerful woman in the room.

Going back to the prisoner, his eyes ran between Lyron and me. "S-so you're a new Leader's whore now? Desmond will cut off his hands for that. No, he will make you burn him alive... ha! That would be-"

The blade flew to his mouth, piercing the skin at the corner, shutting him up. "Shhhh, I am no man's whore. I am his bodyguard, but I doubt he likes you talking that way about me. If you had the smallest sliver of dignity, I would have let you tell Desmond all that you witnessed here, but I have been too merciful. I don't like you, I don't like your nasty little words coming out of your mouth. You smear my name in the mud, but what I did was survive. Perhaps you're a victim too, of Desmond's madness. But in that you turned to destroy lives instead of save them, so to me you're even worse. You sat back and allowed a madman to harness power he had no right to. You disgust me."

The blade moved away before slicing through his vocal cords. Not enough for a quick death. I wanted him to suffer. Watching as he gasped for air, he grabbed at my ankles, trying to beg for me to save him. No one moved as I watched him with uncaring eyes.

Going back to Lyron, I handed his blade back. When I turned back around, Omar was dead. Lyron's voice broke through the silence. "Well, that ended about as well as I thought it would."

"How so?" I asked, looking at Lyron as he took my bloodied hand. My hands were bathed in red.

"I knew you wouldn't like him," he said as he stood up and looked to Thor. "Burn his corpse. We got what we wanted out of him."

"Understood," Thor replied, and he whistled to signal a few men from the crowd to assist. The refugees appeared reassured, and Remi could finally breathe easier. I approached her and Maki as he must have taken over when I lost control. I hardly remembered walking up to him, just his words struck me in anger and that anger won out. The adrenaline was hitting now as I tried to remain calm.

Hands held my shoulders, and I jumped slightly at the touch. Lyron looked at me and his brows pulled together.

Glancing into my eyes, he guided me through the crowd without a word. I didn't have it in me to refuse. One moment I felt in control—the next I was spiraling. My breathing became shallow as we entered Lyron's room and he escorted me to a chair to sit. Looking down at my hands, they were covered in blood, the weight of my actions finally coming down. *Who was that?* It was me, but a part of me locked away, the darkest part.

I vaguely heard water being poured and Lyron's footsteps as he came back to me. "May I touch you?" he asked as he waited for me to nod before taking my hand and washing my arm. He treated me with gentle movements, always moving slowly, as if I'd break.

Maybe I would.

His voice broke through once again, gently and tenderly, as he stopped washing my hands, the now red cloth being replaced by a clean white one. "May I take off your shoes?"

I nodded as he worked slowly and washed my ankles where I was grabbed. The water was warm and comforting as I flexed my toes and ankle.

"I thought I lost you," Lyron said as he rested his forehead on my knee.

"Lost me?" I asked, tilting my head, running my hand through his obsidian black hair.

"The way your eyes looked at me when taking my dagger. I never met that Milana before. I've met much of you, but never the side that was willing to kill a man," he clarified as his hands stopped.

Staying silent for a moment, I continued to run my hand through his hair. It was soft and braided loosely today. Strands escaped more than usual, and I took the time to notice the difference between our skin color. Mine was pale and his was a beautiful tan. The sun's rays did not touch my skin the same as it did his and yet I found the contrast beautiful. He was the man who didn't care that I killed a man in cold blood. He cared about my soul. Not cleaning it, but making sure I came back to him.

"I didn't know what happened. The anger, the sadness, the hate, the frustration, the fear. It all turned me into *that* woman," I said, my voice quivering.

"That woman is a part of you. It doesn't matter, he deserved to die. I would have killed him myself if you found yourself unsure. He had no right to look at you, let alone say anything in your presence. I should have killed him in the dungeon when he said he wanted to see you. But then to see you hold that much strength," he said, tilting his head up, looking into my eyes with his sapphire eyes. "It was worth every moment of doubt. You are a warrior. You are a woman. You are the strongest woman I have ever known."

I opened my mouth to speak, but I couldn't find the words. Standing up, he touched my chin and his thumb brushed against my skin. He lingered a moment before his hand dropped to his side.

"Stay here for the night if you wish. You must be tired and I will be busy with things until the morning," he said. I reached out and grabbed his wrist.

"Please stay," I whispered. "Just until I fall asleep." I didn't know why I wanted him to stay, but being alone felt terrifying.

He nodded as he took my hand and escorted me to his bed. I threw back the covers and tucked myself inside as he laid down on top of the covers beside me, propping his head up to watch me. The exhaustion was overpowering, but I had to ask him what was bothering me. "Why do this for me?"

His voice was sure and left no room to wonder about their meaning. The honesty of his heart pierced through my exhaustion to let me see a piece of his bare soul. "Milana, I would rip apart the world for you if it meant you found peace. I do this because you have given me my humanity back when I thought it was lost. The least I can do is bring you back home. Back to me, even if you do not see me in more than a friendly manner. I meant what I said when I told you I will not have you if you will not have me."

"Thank you," I murmured, gently lifting myself up and pressing my lips to his in a lingering, tender kiss. He remained motionless, and in that moment, the kiss bridged the gap between the warrior I had become and the woman I truly was. It was a kiss that whispered of gratitude, love, and a sense of belonging. I was finally home, thanks to him. Turning to my side, facing away from him, I wore a contented smile and playfully added, "Consider it payback for that unforgettable night at the festival."

Lyron

That little minx, I thought as I saw her smile and turn away. But by the time I was going to say anything, she was already sleeping. I would have Ivy bring her a change of clothes later, and a proper washing basin. Although this was the third time in my bed, I could not call her mine without knowing for sure how she felt.

The kiss could have meant gratitude, or her cocky way of getting back at me. She never ceased to amaze me. Her strength, her words, her wit, her spirit. All of her was magical in a world of gray. The Firan abilities suited her. Passionate, fierce, and loyal. My Airian abilities were becoming entranced by her. Whenever she was around, it was hard to keep it under control, the kiss and how she surprised me in the hall. The wind flared to life as if to keep her blaze alight. I lived to see her rise to the top of her potential.

My life had held little meaning before she entered it, sweeping me into the madness we now faced. But with her, I found a newfound sense of purpose and genuine care for her and her people. In the past, I might have wanted to help but not known how or cared enough to search for answers. She was the vibrant force that had consumed me entirely. I would willingly follow her to the ends of the earth and do whatever she asked, although deep down, I knew she would never ask for such sacrifices. Despite her struggles to comprehend the ways of the Order here and to connect with the people, I had unwavering faith that she would eventually find her way.

I rested the back of my head between her shoulder blades, hearing her breathe deeply and soundly. Hearing the creak of my door, I held up my hand to stop the approacher. Looking up, it was Thor who stared with wide eyes. Standing up, I headed to him and closed the door behind me.

"Yes?"

Thor continued to be silent, then finally, "It is done, Lyron." The corpse had been disposed.

"Thank you," I said as Thor nodded.

Looking at me, the door, then back to me, he cleared his throat. "So, how long have you two been... this?"

"This?"

"Together," he clarified, narrowing his eyes.

"We are not. I simply saw she was in shock and offered her a quiet place to sleep," I responded, shrugging.

"A quiet place to sleep, huh," he said as he shook his head and smiled. Turning around, he headed back down the hall and I followed. "On another note, we should prepare for war if Desmond is truly coming. He could be at our doorstep soon if he thought his men were killed already. It's been a month, so the timeline fits."

"Prepare the scouts for anything. Keep up guard duty but make sure they get enough rest so that when we do have to fight they'll be ready instead of exhausted," I ordered as we approached the main entry room. "Milana will train with Oak and myself. I want her to be prepared for anything they throw at her, she will be their main goal if the claims are correct. Desmond is always obsessed over something, this time it's her."

"So, Desmond is this enigma of crazy and we should just kill on sight pretty much?" Thor looked to me in confusion. He knew of Desmond, but not the level that I did.

"You can tell the scouts that, yes." Seeing the smile on Thor's face as he nodded, made me realize just why we got along so well. As much as we argued, when it came to fighting we tended to be on the same page.

"Excellent. They'll love to hear that. No one messes with one of our own," he said as he took off at a jog to find his scouting team.

No one could understand just what I would do to keep Milana safe.

Out of the corner of my eye, I saw Maki and Remi. Remi's face was red and blotchy from tears.

"Is she okay?" she asked as Maki held her shoulders.

"She's sleeping and cleaned up. She's okay," I said with a nod as Maki let out a breath and Remi smiled.

"Thank you, for saving her."

I swallowed hard, my heart a tumultuous storm of emotions. I fought the urge to confess that I hadn't saved her; in truth, she had rescued me long ago, and now I simply owed her this, even if it meant hiding the truth.

I love her and would do anything for her.

"You're welcome," I managed to say, my voice carrying a hint of the deep affection that bound me to her, before I turned and continued on my way.

CHAPTER 13 WAR

<u>Milana</u>

"Again," Thor called out, his voice unwavering, as he guided me through my training once more.

Oak and Thor maintained a relentless training regimen, pushing me to my limits. They imparted crucial skills, including the art of combat against multiple opponents, making sure I was well-prepared for any situation.

Dripping in sweat and muscles crying out in agony, I groaned and almost let out a snarl. Sunny frowned in the corner, but every time she intervened, they made my sessions even longer. Training was essential. Even the young ones were being taught basic defense and where to hide in the surrounding forests should things take a turn for the worst.

"I hate you so much," I spat out. My fists were in the ready position in front of my chin and nose. I was only fighting Thor since Oak sat by his wife, wiping off his brow with a cloth she'd offered.

"That's fine," Thor shrugged. "Just land a solid hit and we can stop."

Five rounds is what it took. Five agonizing rounds of memorizing his moves that he tried to make seem unpredictable. Eventually there was a pattern. He was good at hiding it.

I went over to Sunny and she handed me a cloth in one hand and a full waterskin in the other. Oak looked at her in surprise. "You didn't tell me you brought water." He almost sounded offended.

"I figured she'd need it more than you," she said, taking in a deep breath and letting it out. "I wasn't wrong."

I smiled and took a long drink of the cool water. "I appreciate that. At least someone cares about my well being," I said as Thor shook his head.

"We are, but Desmond and his men are not going to allow you water breaks," Thor said, gesturing wildly with his hands. A nervous tendency he had.

I nodded in agreement, but I hated his name being brought up to make the point. Obviously, I knew there weren't going to be water breaks. It was just nice to have a female around during these training sessions.

"That was unnecessary," Sunny protested, rising to her feet and placing her hands on her hips, her tone conveying her disapproval.

Oak put his face in his hands as he let his wife go on a tirade about Thor's lack of reading the room. I enjoyed the show. Thor seemed less entertained. However, if anyone knew anything here, it was that Oak was very protective of his wife, and Oak could break a skull with minimal effort. While Sunny could handle herself, she practically married a self aware boulder.

"I'm sorry," Thor said, strained as he looked between me and Sunny. We both just smiled at each other as he looked like he was on his last lifeline, worn out from her outburst.

"Accepted. Now let's get some food," I called out. Sunny bounded next to me as the guys lingered behind.

"So, are you going to tell me about *that* day?" Sunny whispered, referring to when I sliced a man's throat open. According to Thor, the entire Order was aware. With Lyron concentrating on the fortification of the Order, he left truly little to wonder about the opinions of others.

"Nothing to tell. He offered me a quiet place to stay," I said, bumping into her shoulder.

Raising an eyebrow, she poked at my ribs. "In his bed?"

I shook my head. "With my clothes on. At least, mostly, I think my shoes were off."

"Such a tease," she mumbled. "Fine, fine. But I told you he had feelings."

"You did, and he's patient with me." I never admitted my feelings out loud, but then there was a time and place for that. Right now, it doesn't feel right to make it known. But then, I wasn't sure how to define my feelings. I was thankful for him and cared for him, but was that love?

"He better be. If not, let me know and I'll beat him myself," she said, cracking her knuckles with a fierce determination.

I giggled and nodded. "You got it."

Making our way to breakfast, I found I enjoyed my routine here. Training with Oak and Thor in the morning, breakfast with Remi and Maki, talking strategy with Lyron and Thor, training with Lyron in the evening, dinner with Remi and Maki and sometimes Ivy when she wasn't busy helping Kira, and then sleeping. I stayed plenty busy and entertained even with the danger was looming. I felt better now than I did in the past. There were people here to protect, and I thought less of revenge and more of the justice that would be served. The hatred in my heart was slowly replaced with hope, day by day.

Finishing breakfast, I found Lyron in a room by the medical unit used for strategy meetings. The room was lit by torches, along with a candle on the large oval table. Papers were strewn about with numbers that Lyron and Thor compiled during their interrogations over the years and what we knew about Desmond. The fighting force, his psychological manipulation tactics, and his tendencies were thoroughly examined and scrutinized. This included an analysis of how he adapted his methods based on the accounts of Remi and Maki, who had the most recent interactions with him.

"What else is there to go over?" I asked, observing them huddled over the documents, seemingly unaware of my presence.

Lyron looked up, his eyes bloodshot and unable to focus. "I feel I'm missing something. Something obvious and yet hidden. His obsession with you is easy to pinpoint. He's prideful, he loves thinking highly of himself, and uses people's weaknesses against him. His fighting force is dwindling every time he sends them to find you, especially recently. There's no way he could have known when we were leaving. We did a perimeter check, and no one was in sight. Thor did it himself and I double checked. I don't want to think we have a leak somewhere, but..."

"It's the only real option after we rule out the improbable," Thor finished, and Lyron nodded. The exhaustion was evident, but they would not find anything in this condition.

"You need to rest, both of you. If he were to show up today, you'd be sitting ducks. We can reassess tomorrow," I scolded, hands on hips.

Lyron's mouth formed a tired smile and looked at Thor. "She's right. We need our rest. Let's come back to this tonight after some shut eye. Kira and the others will make sure the Order is safe until we wake up." He looked back at me. "Training is off today. I heard you had morning training with Thor and Oak."

"I did."

Putting a hand on my shoulder, he nodded and put his forehead close to mine, only a couple of stray hairs grazing my skin. "Then you rest as well, or go for a dip in the lake. It's hot today." The summer had been blistering the last couple of days, sunshine raging down with little comfort even with the trees. The air was thick and hot, barely fun to fight in. But for me it was only a discomfort. Life in the desert was a breeze compared to this.

"Don't worry, go rest," I said, locking eyes with him. I could sense his concern, evident in the lines on his face. His apprehension never ceased, yet he never voiced it directly. *Or I could join you,* lingered in my thoughts as a potential course for the evening. The idea momentarily diverted my attention, and although invasive, it wasn't an unwelcome one.

They walked away, and I took a moment to review the papers on the table. Thor and Desmond briefly crossed paths at the Mountain Order. I could testify that as a fact. However, Desmond was extreme, even for them. There was consideration he may have had some old friends there that stayed back when he went to the Desert Order. I remember him arriving with a small following. Maybe three men.

Lyron was still vague about how he knew him besides having fought together. I wondered if there was more to it for this much animosity. My hatred made sense; he killed my friends and family like they were ants beneath his feet and wanted me for my power. For Lyron to hate him just as much, I was curious just what had triggered that desperation. A difference in values was one thing, but if it was personal...

I continued to wonder until I saw the paper trail of victims, alive or passed, that we knew about. Remi, Ivy, and myself were listed. There was another name there I didn't recognize. Tune.

I saw she was in the Mountain Order, a young woman with Terran abilities. Known associate of Lyron and Thor in scouting. Intelligent. Dead by Desmond when she refused him. That was all the information laid out about her. For some inexplicable reason, her profile held the greatest fascination for me among the handful that there were. Of course, Desmond had killed many more, but only a few of us had actual profiles written out. Among them, only two had profiles dedicated to deceased victims: my brother, Cyrus, and now Tune.

I shook my head, trying to not get too invested in the idea that Thor and Lyron were keeping secrets. They were allowed to, but this one bothered me. Like a small rock in my shoe that refused to go away.

Thinking of my time here, I realized how many things had changed. Initially serving as bait to draw Desmond out, the possibility of me becoming a bodyguard seemed to be an integral part of that overall plan. It was going around to neighboring Orders that a woman Firan was guarding the Leader of Eagle Point Order. Even our old friend, Tank, brought some of his friends from the Northern Order to help us fortify our forces.

As I left the room, I was greeted with waves and hellos as I walked back to the entrance to see if my help was needed elsewhere. It struck me how effortlessly I now smiled and waved, a far cry from the nervousness that had consumed me for the longest time, particularly after my altercation with Kira, which now felt like a distant memory. I had finally found a place to call home.

Lyron

I watched Milana as she helped the women pull up water from the well to store it deeper inside the fortress, just in case Desmond's forces should try to poison our water. The animals were being built shelters inside and we harvested what we could. Should he try anything, we would be ready. As much as Milana wanted me to rest, I could not. There was too much to do, but being lost in my thoughts was not an option either.

Thor had been at my door for a moment before he knocked. I knew what he wanted to talk about. That didn't mean it made it easier.

"Do you miss her?" he asked quietly as he shut the door behind him.

My breath hitched as I remembered the woman I loved all those years ago. At least was infatuated with if nothing else. "I do sometimes. Other times I forget her. Does that make me cruel?"

Thor joined me, glancing in the direction my gaze was fixed. "Not necessarily, just means you're alive, and she's not. Hard to remember someone you haven't seen in years. Especially when someone else is in front of you."

I looked to Thor as he looked at the moon on the horizon, all the broken pieces shimmering against the blue sky. "Do you still hate me for what happened?"

Thor shook his head and the corner of his mouth upturned for a moment. "I would have killed you long ago if that were the case. Tune was the only family I had left, and because of your interference and Desmond's, she died. I followed you to plan my revenge because what you didn't kill her, but your actions led to that result." He stared at Milana and the way she smiled as she worked with the other women. "Goddess, she looks like her, doesn't she? If she had lighter colored hair. Even acts like her. I think it helps me to remember her sometimes."

I nodded, remembering how she appeared in the woods. Her fierce nature reminded me of Tune's strength and stubbornness. Now I saw two vastly different women. I realized Thor was acquainted with a side of Tune that as her older brother, I was not privy to. Maybe how Cyrus saw Milana had he been alive.

"Thank you for staying here and building this Order with me. Thanks to you, we made a home for many people who are suffering because of Desmond, and not killing him. Because of that sin, we allowed countless others to die." I closed my eyes and regretted that day every moment of my life. "Because we couldn't do what had to be done. Milana suffered and yet she doesn't hate us for it. I couldn't tell myself to just tell her how I felt, and now I wonder if I'll ever get to. If it means dying, I will kill Desmond. But if that happens, will you tell her to live happily? Will you make sure of it?"

"I'll tell her, but you should tell her yourself," Thor said as he clasped his hand on my shoulder. After he left my room, I sat in a chair and hung my head, closing my eyes. All those lives. I looked at my hands. They were golden from the sun and yet all I could see was crimson stains of blood.

Moving my hands in a swirling motion, I created a twist of air that sustained for a few moments before dissipating. Closing my fist, I decided it was time to show Desmond a trick up my sleeve when he arrived. As much as we were preparing for an army, I had a feeling he would be arrogant enough to come alone. He always thought no one could touch him, but I also knew he would have his men waiting to attack anyone who ran in the forest. As nightfall approached, the possibility of us becoming surrounded loomed larger, particularly if the scouts detecting movement along the mountain base were indeed linked to Desmond's advances.

Closing my eyes once meant I could see Tune and remember the way her face would blush when my hands would caress her cheek and told her she was beautiful. Sweet words and simple touches were all that happened between us. Desmond wanted her, and she wanted me. I wasn't there to defend her one night, and he took the only thing he could. She tried to kill him, so he killed her with a rock to the skull.

Now when I close my eyes, I don't see Tune. I see Milana smiling by the lake as she goes swimming with Sunny and Remi. I see her laughing at dinner with Ivy. Her determination in her training. The way her face turns red when I stare at her too long, not saying a word. The way her lips felt that night of the festival, and again when she killed a man.

That night, I felt her soul calling out to be saved. As if being a point of no return. What motivated me to be so gentle was not only out of adoration, but respect for her as a person. Slowly, I felt her come back to me. To watch her go that far away was frightening, but I knew I would do far worse to keep her safe if anyone tried to harm her.

Her flame is mine to protect from afar. To allow her to live freely and be with me if she so desires. Nevertheless, my unwavering commitment is to protect her, a choice I make willingly.

Opening my eyes, I thought I was hallucinating when I saw her standing in front of me.

"You seem lost in a dream, even if you are standing up," she said, reaching for my hand. Holding it gently, she reached up with her other hand and held my cheek.

"If it's a dream, it's a good one." I smiled as she blushed. I felt the flinch in her hand before she would take it away. I turned my hand and nestled my mouth against her palm.

We stood there in silence. Waiting for everything and nothing.

"How did you...?"

"The window. I wanted to know if I could climb it," she said, so innocently curious. A smile spread across her face and I leaned forward to embrace her before Thor abruptly opened my doors.

"He's here. The scouts saw him entering the forest, and the forest is quiet. No doubt he has... reinforcements." He slowed when he saw Milana and I.

"Sound the alarm. Get all the scouts in for watch duty. No doubt if we send anyone out to the forest, they will pick off our men and women. Get everyone inside. Only Kira, you and I should greet our guest with the welcome he deserves. An unwelcomed one."

Milana nodded as she took my hand. It did not tremble out of fear. That was obvious from the way she didn't flinch. The tremble I felt was the anticipation. The months of training, years of trauma, moments of self doubt, all leading up to this moment.

"Are you ready?" I asked her.

"Yes," she said, her voice sure.

Thor nodded and left the room. His lingering gaze reminded me to tell her. But...

"When this is over, I want you to know something. Promise me you'll let me tell you," I said, afraid she would be distracted by how I truly felt about her.

"Of course," she said with a quick nod before letting go of my hand. "You can tell me anything when this is over."

Anything... I wanted to tell her more than life itself.

Following behind Milana, I heard the rushing of feet in the halls as people were guided to the bowels of the fortress. The many safety measures we took would ensure their survival. Everyone knew not to be out in the open. The archers they had would no doubt be ready to take anyone foolish enough to underestimate them. We would be in the main entry area where I had my stone chair upon the dais. Milana veered off to help the women and children get to safety, making sure everyone had what they needed.

As I sat in anticipation, I heard the whistles that signaled Desmond's approaching footsteps at varying distances. Just then, Maki appeared before me, and I couldn't help but wonder about his sudden arrival.

"Protect Milana, will you? That son of a bitch took everything and last time I saw her kill a man who did us all wrong, I was happy and yet..." His voice hitching, I understood what he meant. It was hard to watch someone die, let alone watching someone we care about become the executioner.

"You have my word," I said as he looked up with tears in his eyes.

"Thank you. I will protect the people here with my life should it come to that so long as you keep that promise." He turned and jogged down the hall.

He was a good kid. Thor admired him and Maki aspired to be like Thor. An admirable goal. While Thor and I may not have always gotten along, I always admired that magnetic personality and charisma he had. While I lived in darkness, he lived in the light. He could be the hero for the Order while I did what I had to do.

The sun was setting by the time I heard the whistle indicating that Desmond was emerging from the forest. Kira and Milana made their way to me, and Thor was not far behind.

"Everyone is secure," Kira said with a nod. "I'll be in my perch with my arrows."

"Thank you," I said to Kira as Milana put her hand on my forearm. Thor went to my other side. Kira patted Milana on the shoulder and jogged away before she could be seen.

Meant to be a last resort, it was reassuring that she would be keeping an eye on things above while we took care of the main problem here.

"Are you sure you want to be here?" I inquired, my hand finding hers. The fiery determination in her gaze left no room for uncertainty. The closure she yearned for, the reassurance she sought. It was all here in this moment, unspoken yet deeply understood. "Then we will do what must be done." Her nod conveyed unwavering commitment.

The trees rustled as Desmond emerged from the greenery wearing a broad smile, extending his arms in greeting. "Hello, my dear Milana. I came to bring you home."

"Home?" Milana spat. "I wouldn't go back with you if you were the last man on this earth, Desmond."

Desmond's face turned from a smile to a snarl in the blink of an eye. "You'll regret those words, my love."

"Your love?" I scoffed. "You're a psychotic tyrant, Desmond. She was never yours to begin with."

Desmond laughed, the sound sending shivers down my spine. "I have no need to justify myself to you. But know this, I will take what I want, and what I want is Milana."

In that moment, Milana stepped forward, flames leaping from her fingertips. Desmond didn't flinch, but I could see the fear in his eyes.

"You can try, Desmond, but you will fail," I threatened, my voice low and rumbling.

Desmond's eyes flicked to me, and his hand moved to the sword at his belt. "I suppose we'll see about that, won't we? Maybe Tune would have survived had you been with her that night, Lyron."

Milana and I stepped forward, readying ourselves for what was to come. Desmond was a skilled fighter, but we were both determined to stand our ground. Thor moved closer to us, ready to protect us both if things turned sour.

Desmond unsheathed his sword, its steel glinting in the fading light. "The two of you together couldn't defeat me," he said, sneering.

I smirked. "Maybe not alone, but together, we're unstoppable."

Milana nodded in agreement, her eyes still flickering with flames.

Desmond charged towards us, sword raised high. I summoned a gust of wind, but Desmond was too quick, dodging the attack with ease. Milana hurled a ball of fire, but it merely grazed his arm, leaving a small burn. Her eyes widened towards me, but now, we had to be united.

Desmond swung his sword at me, who evaded the attack and countered with a swift kick, sending Desmond reeling backwards. Milana took advantage of the distraction and unleashed a barrage of fireballs, each one more powerful than the last.

But Desmond was not so easily defeated. He deftly dodged the attacks, his sword flashing through the air. It was clear he had the upper hand in terms of fighting skill, but Milana and I had something he did not—the power of the elements.

I summoned a powerful gust of wind, which sent Desmond hurtling backwards. Milana took the opportunity to unleash a massive inferno, which engulfed him in flames. For a moment, it looked like we had won.

But as the smoke cleared, we saw that Desmond was still standing. The flames had merely singed his clothes, and his eyes were burning with rage.

"You think a little fire and wind can defeat me?" he snarled. "You have no idea what you're up against."

Desmond charged us, his sword raised high. I summoned another gust of wind, hoping to knock him off balance, but he merely shrugged it off. Milana tried to blast him with fire, but he was too fast, deflecting the attack with his sword. Seeing that my own attacks were useless, I decided to try something different. Suddenly, the very air around Desmond began to twist and contort. He stumbled, an expression of bewilderment crossing his face. Then, in an instant, he was lifted off the ground and propelled backward, as if an unseen force had seized his ankles and flung him through the air. Desmond landed with a crash, his sword clattering to the ground. For a moment, he lay there, stunned. Then he began to struggle to his feet, his eyes blazing with fury.

"You'll pay for that," he growled.

But before he could rise fully, Milana was upon him. She summoned a massive ring of fire enclosing him in a burning vortex. He thrashed and screamed as she continued to send wave after wave until she was nearly falling over from the effort.

Going to her, I put my hand on her shoulders and moved them down to cover her fingers with mine. Closing my eyes, I moved the wind to keep her flames going. His screams became more tormented and when she saw him drop to his knees, only then did she stop her assault.

His skin was warped around his arms and back. He must have shielded himself, but his clothes were nearly falling off, and smoke poured from him.

"You bastard, Airian," he sneered as I approached him.

"That's right, I am a bastard. I should have killed you long ago to save so many others from your pitiful excuse for revenge. Is that what this was about?" I asked, kneeling on the other side of the flames.

I once saw him as a brother in arms, and yet now all I saw was nothing more than madness and death.

He chuckled, although he coughed and winced in pain. He continued, "Revenge? What a pitiful thing. No, this was about wanting it all." He looked at Milana, and I stepped in front of him. "The flames of war are a beautiful thing. She will bring war, even if she doesn't lead it herself."

"You don't deserve to even say her name," I growled and Milana stepped to my side.

"Sad," she said, looking down at him with disgust. "I remember being so afraid of you. Now, I see a sad little man. I want you to rot in the dungeon with darkness as your only ally. You deserve death, but only when you beg for it."

I looked to her strength in admiration. Her desire for his death to now wanting to truly have him experience what he did to others.

"Ah, but my dear... then I'll never tell you about how Cyrus escaped me. I know where the rat has been, but he's not the same." Milana seized him by the throat, and I observed with caution, while Thor stood at the ready.

"How dare you speak his name!" she screamed. Tears threatened to fall, but she willed them back. "You will rot. I will not be lured by your deceptions and lies. Your men will be hunted and killed one by one. I will see to it that you are nothing but dust in the wind in the sands of history." She dropped him and looked to Thor. "Lock him away. Assure the perimeter is safe. We will go hunting for the rest after."

Thor and I took Desmond to the dungeons, and he twisted and turned in our grasp. Too weak to make a significant impact, we threw him in the deepest cell we could after circling around different passages. Even if he had someone try to rescue him, they would get lost. Making our way out, Milana was waiting.

She pulled back her fist and hit me square in the jaw. My eyes widened from the shock as I tasted blood.

"Milana, I don't understand," I said, shaking my head.

"An Airian! You didn't think to tell me." Milana glared at me and Thor. "Did you know?"

He nodded and she pulled back to punch him. Letting her do so, he stumbled back. Not the first time he had been hit by her from what I heard, but then her training paid off.

"Who's Tune?" she asked, full of rage. The papers, she must have seen the papers. Then Desmond had brought up her name.

"She was my sister, and in love with Lyron." Thor spat out blood, his teeth were covered in red. "Desmond killed her in jealousy."

Milana nodded and walked away. I felt my heart sink when she stumbled and fell to her knees. An arrow had pierced her between her shoulder blades.

The sound of Kira's screams pierced the air, and when I looked up, I saw Kira shoving a man off the fortress's edge. His bow and arrows struck the ground before his body thudded against the stone. My eyes were fixed on Milana in a state of panic as I rushed to her side. Amidst the chaos, I heard another scream, a deep and unending one.

I was the one screaming.

CHAPTER 14 FIND ME

<u>Milana</u>

Remi was at my bedside, in tears. I had been out for a few days, the remaining few I refused to see anyone. My wounds were healed, my body ready to help hunt Desmond's men. Reports they had escaped to the Mountain Order bothered me. For all of Lyron's and Thor's secret keeping, you'd think they could do one job right.

"Please, have something to eat," Remi pleaded, as I had been steadfast in my refusal to eat for the past few days since I woke up, and I also resisted the urge to sleep.

I was bitter. I was angry. I was hurt.

It was irrational, but I couldn't help it. The thought of Tune being in his life infuriated me. Immature, *yes*. I had been with men, but it didn't matter to me. Tune had a hold of his heart. I saw it in the way his demeanor changed when Desmond said *her* name.

Knowing he could control air... that was surprising, but I understood. His power was more rare than mine. Aggravating but tolerable. Keeping that large of a secret from me about why he and Thor mutually hated Desmond was beyond my capacity to handle rationally. I hated myself for hating him, but the churning of emotions didn't stop.

The trust that I thought we had felt small and insignificant now instead of the crutch I used as we fought Desmond. I felt alive when fighting alongside Lyron. As if that was the place I was born to be. In that moment, the flame within me yearned for him. Yearning for his acceptance of my destructive power, my unyielding journey of self worth, and even accepting that I was ready to be with him.

It wasn't hate that consumed me; it was a potent mix of jealousy and heartache. I couldn't bring myself to hate him, not when I witnessed him lifting me off the ground, his tears pleading for me not to abandon him. Tears welled up in my eyes, and Remi paused as she reached out to me. Despite my flinching, she remained undeterred. "You're hurt?" she asked, and I shook my head.

"No," I sobbed.

"Thor told me about Tune. Is that what this is about?" she asked tenderly, taking my hand and sitting closer to me.

"Yes," I sobbed again as I leaned into her and let my tears out.

A flood of emotions poured out of me. Desmond was now a prisoner, and I almost died. Lyron and Thor kept secrets from me, when I had bared everything. I felt lost and confused, just like when I escaped into the desert with nothing but hope to hold on to all those years ago.

"Oh, Milana," she whispered as she hugged me close. "It was too much, wasn't it?"

I didn't answer. The pain and confusion that came out of my body in the form of powerful sobs lasted for what seemed like forever. At least until I must have fallen asleep. I heard voices some time later in the dark.

"She just went to sleep. Please, let her rest," Remi's voice pleaded, although slightly muffled.

"Please, just let me see her," Lyron pleaded from just beyond my closed door. I suspected Remi was with him since I couldn't see her, but my door remained shut.

"You didn't tell her. What did you think was going to happen? It may not have seemed important to you, but to her it feels like betrayal. Like you didn't trust her like she trusted you."

A long pause. Too long. I thought he had gone away until I heard his voice break in pain.

"I know. I have to make things right with her. So, please let her know I'd still like to tell her something important. Like I promised I would."

Those words hit hard. He did promise to tell me something after the fight. Was that it? Was he going to tell me about Tune... about how he felt about us?

A part of me wanted to know everything, but another was afraid to uncover the tarnished image I had of him. The image of a Leader who genuinely cared, who refused to let anyone perish if he could prevent it, who mourned when one of his people passed away while continuing to be their pillar of support, the man who wiped the blood from my hands and kept me close. That was the man who I wanted, but I knew if I wanted to truly know him, I had to know who he was before Eagle Point Order. And for him to know me, he had to know about me.

That terrified me.

I heard his footsteps fade down the hall. She opened the door and pity radiated from her. The words didn't need to be exchanged, but she couldn't help but leave one piece of my heart bleeding on the floor. Disappointment coated her words like acid to my skin. "He cares for you, you know. I'm not going to sit here and keep watching you be foolish. I'm heading down to breakfast. Sit here in your wallowing for all I care."

She shut the door with a sudden thud and left me to wallow. The light from my window shone through brightly, drawn to it. The people below all had a story I was a part of now. Before, I could keep that separate. Now, they were equally a part of me. Beyond into the forest, I knew Desmond's men were still waiting. Many of them were captured or killed, but not all of them. We had to prepare for a real war should it come down to it. If one of

Desmond's men took over the Mountain Order in a challenge, it would mean trouble. We needed reinforcements, too.

In that moment, I realized how vulnerable we truly were. Beyond the safety of these walls lay an impending danger - Desmond's men lurking in wait like shadows in the forest. Some had already fallen, but others remained out there, ready for battle should it come to that. Fear gripped at my heart as I contemplated what would happen if one of them seized control over our Order. It would mean chaos and destruction - something we desperately needed reinforcements for. And I needed answers for. Tank and the Northern Order was a solid force, but if the Desert Order was no longer under Desmond's control, maybe there was a resistance left...

What if Cyrus was alive? The thought ate at me slowly, like a poison. I had to know.

Leaving my room, I snuck through the corridors and into the dungeons. The cool, stale air was musty and pungent the further I went. The darkness was overpowering, feeling like anyone could be there. Even thinking I heard steps behind me. I had to ground myself to keep my thoughts from going rampant. I felt lost for hours; this dungeon was unending.

Finally, I heard breathing. It stopped when my footsteps drew near.

His voice was calm and steady. It bothered me. "Is that you, Reaper?"

Reaper? I shook my head to myself and cleared my throat.

"Ah, no. The flames of war, my mouse."

Anger flared up in me. "I am not your mouse. And you owe me an explanation."

"About Cyrus?" His calm demeanor only threatened to make me lose mine. I had to keep a calm head if I was going to survive this conversation with some piece of my sanity. "A bargain for information?"

"What do you want?" I seethed at him.

"A message to your Leader. A message that says 'They've always been here.' He will know what it means," he said as my eyes opened. *Spies.* Panic ensued, but he owed me. "I will tell you about Cyrus next time we meet. Please let your master know he should keep me alive, though."

I ran through the dungeons. I stumbled and collapsed multiple times. By the time I escaped, it was well into the afternoon. Thor was ahead of me and stormed towards me with anger.

"What the hell were you doing? We have been looking everywhere for you," he said before seeing my face in panic.

"I had to know about my brother. But I need to talk to Lyron now. Desmond has spies here and I feel like something tragic will happen soon," I whispered urgently.

"Shit, he's in the forest thinking you needed space. I'll go find him. Talk to Kira. She should be in the medical unit," he said as he ran towards the forest.

As I ran to the medical unit, the glares punctured me. Remi told me how the refugees were not pleased with Desmond existing this close to their new home. Many of them were threatening to leave if he should stay alive for long. I didn't blame them, but I needed to know about Cyrus. I needed to know I was still human after all the thoughts of revenge. Justice felt far better served, and yet the unease lingered like a sore. This revelation made that sore blister.

Kira was helping a young man who just joined the scouts and eyed me suspiciously when I came into the unit, out of breath. Excusing herself, she told the man to change out of his dressing tomorrow or come back to see her if he was unsure of how to do it. He nodded and left the room quickly. I shut the door tight and glanced around.

"What's going on?" she asked, putting a hand on my shoulder.

"I talked to Desmond and..."

"You, WHAT?"

My words came together as a plea. I didn't know where to start and if he always had them here, then who knew who the spies could be. "Yes, I know, but he said he has spies here. That he always has. Do you know of anyone who could want to help him? Anyone that could have slipped by from the Mountain Order, or a refugee?"

She shook her head, her eyes widening at the realization. "I don't know. I'll try to put together any strange activity, but with all the ones we've taken in, I haven't been able to talk to them as much as I should have."

"Okay, keep an eye out. Thor knows, and he's getting Lyron. I hope this isn't a wild chase to make us panic, but I feel something is off. It's too quiet. He came alone, he went down almost too willingly. As if he... wanted..."

Someone did follow me when I went into the dungeons. I wasn't losing it.

"I have to go. Make sure you talk to Thor and Lyron," I said, running full speed back to the dungeon. I needed to know.

Panic ran through me as I approached the dungeon entrance. Only a few steps in, I collided with a body and screamed. Taking steps back, I saw a familiar glint of hair, but with red.

Thor. Covered in blood.

His voice was strained. "He's gone. Escaped. I tried to get him, but he had help." Collapsing to the ground, I cradled his head and yelled for help. I thought he was going to get Lyron? What happened for him to go find Desmond instead? My thoughts collided with each other and suddenly Lyron was in front of me as tears streamed down my face.

"He's hurt," my voice crumbled out as I tried to find the source of the bleeding. Inflicting wounds were more my specialty rather than healing them, and for once I wish I would have paid more attention to the art.

"Help me get him to Kira," he said as he took his torso and I lifted his feet. People whispered as we rushed by; they didn't know what was happening, and I wanted so desperately to tell them all to hide. However, Thor needed to get better. We needed him. I needed him.

Kira dropped her bandages as we approached, with Thor in tow. "Second room on the right. Take off his shirt. I'll be right there." She called out for another woman, and we did as we were told. Lyron ripped open his shirt with ease. He was stabbed in the back. The heat rose in my body as I realized that someone who we knew must have done this.

"Where the hell is Ivy?" Kira called out.

Ivy... no. It couldn't be. She had been here with Kira for days. She'd helped me, taken care of me. I shook my head in denial. I was paranoid and jumping to conclusions.

Lyron's voice broke my thoughts. "You need to come with me," he whispered as Kira and another woman I didn't know worked on Thor. "There's nothing more we can do. Let Kira work."

I shook my head, but he didn't take that as an answer. "Do you want to burn down the fortress, or are you going to pretend you're not seething right now?"

I realized an inferno was raging. I wanted to let it out, but I couldn't here. Not if I wanted to kill people I cared about. Nodding my head, he guided me back to his room.

"Milana, what in the hell?" he said, rubbing his hand through his hair. "Did we do the right thing?"

I shook my head with tears threatening to fall. "I don't know. I don't know." I repeated the words as he came to me and took my face in his hands.

His eyes only asked once, and I closed mine in acceptance. His mouth collided with mine and my world erupted. In that electrifying moment, Desmond's memory fled to the recesses of my mind, Thor's suffering faded into insignificance, and the sole focus of my desires bore upon this enigmatic man before me. Desperation surged forth from deep within, my fingers clutching onto his arms and chest, as if trying to anchor myself to this intoxicating reality.

"You consume me," he breathed as his tongue trailed down my throat.

I swallowed as I leaned my head back, closing my eyes. Savoring his touch as his hands slowed removing my clothing piece by piece as if I would break, as if I would run.

"It's what fire does," I said as I brought my head up and moved so I could remove his clothing. "I consume without caring about what I leave in my wake. It's my burden. But I want you more than anything. You make me feel"-

He cut me off with another passionate kiss. *Alive.*

"Damn the world for being so burnable, then," he murmured against my skin his hands gripped my hips to move me under him. I smiled at his response and the last barriers between us shattered.

While the timing was the worst, this felt right. My flame and his wind collided together and merged into a perfect storm of passion. Wildfire surged through me as he pushed me to the highest point of pleasure.

Laying together afterward in a heap of exhausted limbs, I felt the tension we had between us disperse. I wanted to know about him, but I also wanted to know what he thought of me. He cared for me, wanted me more than anyone else, and yet I hardly knew him. At that moment, sleep was not what I wanted, but it was what I needed.

Sleeping in his arms felt like the truest moment of my life. And yet, I felt so broken inside. Desmond baited me and it allowed someone to follow me in. Thor must have wanted to be sure that no one was inside before running after Lyron and got himself caught. The thought woke me up, along with voices. Kira was talking outside the room with Lyron.

Kira's voice was calm, but urgent. "He will make it. The scouts will follow Desmond's movements at a distance. I would join them soon, or...?"

Lyron thought for a moment before continuing. "I have a plan. It's a long shot but let them know to continue."

Lyron came back inside the room as I pulled the blanket up to cover my chest. His expression looked torn. Pleased to see me in his bed, displeased with the turn of events.

"I always thought when I had you in my bed that it would be a more joyous occasion," he admitted.

"I know what you mean," I said as he sat next to me, his chest bear with only his pants on.

His hand covered mine and his eyes bore into mine with pure adoration. "You're the most beautiful woman I have ever seen. I'm sorry you had to find out about things the way you did. I will tell you everything, but right now, I need to ask you to trust me." I nodded, and he continued. "I think he may be right about your brother. I remember he used to hood up his victims. Was that true with your brother?"

I desperately wanted to believe it, but it was hard to undo years of seeing that moment. "Yes, he hooded him, but the man looked just like him. Body type, height, weight, and even sounded like him."

He nodded. "I know. We should go back to the Desert Order to get clues. When I asked Remi, she believes the same thing you did, and she was never led to believe anything different. But Desmond likes a bargaining chip. He told you to come find me, didn't he?"

"Yes," my voice cracked. "He told me to tell you 'they've always been here'."

"Exactly like that?" he asked cautiously. I nodded. He looked at me and shook his head. "Shit."

The realization struck him like a lightning bolt, causing him to spring to his feet, his hands instinctively flying to his face. In the wake of his mounting frustration, a primal growl of exasperation burst forth, its intensity reverberating throughout the room, causing me to involuntarily shrink back. He channeled his fury into an explosive exhalation, directing it towards the wall on the far side, resulting in a chaotic whirlwind that left papers strewn and a chair contorted beyond repair in its wake.

After a moment, he inhaled deeply, and as he exhaled, the agony etched across his features came into focus. His eyes met mine, filled with an anguish that cut to the core.

"Ivy."

To be continued

THANK YOU FOR READING!

Enjoy Wild Order? Come back for more when book two releases!

Burning Order

Kindle Vella in episode format beginning 2024 followed by a full book release.

Please consider leaving a review on Goodreads, Amazon, or other platforms!

Find all my links here and ways to support me

linktr.ee/sjclements

THE WORLD OF WILD ORDER

The Calamity changed the World, now the World must fight to survive. The way they do this is in Orders, groups of people in settlements varying in region and resources.

Rules of the Orders: (most vary, but these are the overall accepted)

I. The strongest rule. Challenges of hierarchy are a daily occurrence at times depending on the Order. Some (Eagle Point Order, Earth, and Oasis) have festivals to do so to make it less frightening. Mostly those festivals are just fun fighting tournaments if no one challenges the Leader (or those below them) of the Order.

II. Women and children are not to be harmed. With the population dwindled, they are kept the safest. Desert Order does not respect this rule. To bear a child is seen as sacred and ceremonies signal when women are turning of age. However, it is only if they are ready, not necessarily at a specific age.

III. Trade is widely accepted for other items and goods. However, there are certain alliances. For example: Eagle Point Order trades with Northern Order and Mountain Order and seasonally Ocean Order for fish. Lyron is a fair leader and will only hold back trade if there's an ethical disagreement such as with the Desert Order.

The Orders and Some Leaders

Eagle Point Order – This Order is near a large river and has four seasons. They keep crops and farmland and trade with select Orders, such as Mountain Order that resides south, and the Northern Orders in colder climates.

Lyron – main role to keep peace within the Order, seen as the main leader.

Thor- main role to scout the land for any intruders, second in command.

Kira- helping the needs of the women and children, third in command.

Desert Order- Relying on limited food, and creative irrigation to stay alive, their leader is ruthless and keeps them mostly isolated from the East. However, refugees are escaping little by little because of the harsh conditions. Favoring trying death as opposed to life under Desmond.

Desmond- the dictator ruler who takes what he wants by force.

Omar- main role to hunt down Milana and bring her back to Desmond through any means necessary. Last he heard, Milana was running around as a Wild which makes many women his target as it is mostly women who are considered a Wild to gather intel and torture.

Wild- people who live outside of an Order as nomads. There are not very many and that's why Omar is hunting down women Wild.

Ivy – Former Wild, tortured for days as Omar wanted to find Milana, however she knew nothing, just passed through the same area too close together. Found by Thor and now helps Eagle Point Order as needed.

Milana – Wild staying at Eagle Point Order, formerly part of Desert Order

Mountain Order known for their metals and gems. Along with their hearty guardsmen. Known to harbor Desmond's men when traveling.

Earth Order overall, peaceful with the most people to care for. Trades building materials for other resources. In alliance with Eagle Point Order due to their mutual distrust of Desmond

Ocean Order has the best fish harvest and carefree lifestyle.

Oasis Order is isolated, and little is known. No one usually leaves the island or ventures to it.

Northern Order is made up of outcasts from other Orders. Seen as a rebellious group with their leader changing every few years at best, a few days at its worst. However, Lyron knows many of their civilians and keeps things civil between the two Orders.

Snow Fall Order is made up of mostly young women who left many of the orders for one reason or another. Mostly those who were abused by men, they seek solitude and rarely trade. Their location makes it easier to harvest fish and sustain some crops. Usually only trade with Ocean Order when a winter has been rough.

Travel

Horse in mountains is common, dog pulled sled in Northern regions, sand sails in Desert when wind is right (newly developed in recent years), walking by foot is still the most common.

Elemental Abilities

Firan – Fire -Desert Order men are some of the few to have this ability. Women, commonly, do not.

Airian- Air (wind) – The rarest kind. No rhyme or reason for gender or region.

Aquan – Water – Mostly women from the Ocean and Oasis Order.

Terran – Earth – Most common ability between both genders and regions.

ACKNOWLEDGEMENTS

Where to even start...

My husband, the reason I was able to pursue writing and had the motivation to keep this up. This book would not be here without your hard work behind the scenes helping with my emotional moments.

My cousin Jen, you are such a light in this world and such an inspiration.

My Mom, thank you for letting me do what I love without judgement, even if I drive you nuts.

To my friends who read this book and had to deal with hearing so much about Milana, Lyron, Thor, Desmond, and Ivy. And all the changes as I evolved as a writer and the story just got where it is. You are the best.

To my editor, Jennifer Bussell, thank you for loving my enemies to lovers trope and all my craziness.

To my beta readers Erica and Kayla, thank you for your honest feedback!

ABOUT THE AUTHOR

SJ Clements has a Master of the Arts in Creative Writing graduate from SNHU as of 2023. With her nose in a book or writing a story, there are always ideas emerging. Morally grey heroes and heroines thrill her, but variety is the spice of life. Manga, YA, contemporary adult, historical fiction, romance, science fiction line her bookshelves. Most days SJ finds herself playing Final Fantasy, reading a book, or listening to music when not writing.

Wild Order is her debut novel.

Also by SJ Clements

Feeling a Feeling Poetry Collection

(Sarah Clements)

Coming soon

Burning Order

Fall 2024

Wild Order book three – currently unnamed

Spring 2025

www.ingramcontent.com/pod-product-compliance
Lightning Source LLC
Chambersburg PA
CBHW021240060726
47590CB00005B/1834